advance praise
STONE AND STE

"*Stone and Steel* is a sharp and sexy story of love, loyalty and magic. Eboni has given us a world where Black Queerness reigns supreme, and our world is better for it."
— Danny Lore, co-author of *Queen of Bad Dreams*

"An intimate story of cruelty, love, and duty bound up in an immensely lush and complicated magical world, one far bigger than the story can even hint at. You won't forget Odessa and Aaliyah, and you won't forget their people."
— Premee Mohamed, author of *Beneath the Rising*

"*Stone and Steel* is an ambitious, sexy, gloriously fucked-up, genius epic fantasy (somehow) packed into a novella. Aaliyah's story enchanted me, and I'm waiting with bated breath to see what Eboni Dunbar does next."
—Lina Rather, author of *Sisters of the Vast Black*

"The plot is riveting, and readers will cheer for the cast of well-rounded Black characters, led by underdog Aaliyah, as they fights for her people. This will be an easy pick for anyone looking for queer, Black speculative fiction—and for fantasy fans more broadly."
—Publishers Weekly

Neon Hemlock Press
www.neonhemlock.com
@neonhemlock

© 2020 Eboni Dunbar

Stone and Steel
Eboni Dunbar

This novella is entirely a work of fiction. Names,
characters, places and incidents are the products of
the author's imagination or are used fictitiously. Any
resemblance to actual events, locales, organizations or
persons, living or dead, is entirely coincidental.

Cover Illustration by Odera Igbokwe / www.odera.net
Cover Design by dave ring

ISBN-13: 978-1-952086-05-2

Eboni Dunbar
STONE AND STEEL

Neon Hemlock Press

THE 2020 NEON HEMLOCK NOVELLA SERIES

NEON HEMLOCK

Stone
and Steel

BY EBONI DUNBAR

To Roshni Scott.

You love me like none other and that love allows me to create worlds.

I'm lucky to have you in my life.

ONE

A aliyah's army stood on the precipice of home. Soldiers and mages in nearly equal numbers, all of them trained to bring glory to the kingdom of Titus. To Odessa. They were tired, they were hungry, and many of them were injured. They had gathered just around the mountain bend, before they could glimpse the capital city. While they awaited, the river captivated them, the bright blue of the blessed waters amid the green trees, like thousands of emerald clad warriors themselves, as they waited for their general to tell them they could finally go home.

When the ground shifted beneath their feet, making some of the horses jump nervously, General Aaliyah knew that her runner had reached the city. Aaliyah closed her eyes, imagining the way the wall of rock would disappear into the ground, the power it would take to do it. It took great magical strength, tens of her stone mages, but still they made it look so easy. And it was the sign that General Aaliyah had been waiting for.

"Let's get this shit over with," Aaliyah muttered to herself, stretching. Her body still ached from the final battle in the southern isles, and three weeks of riding hadn't helped. She shouldered her spear and prayed for a moment of peace so she could rest her weary body. "Let's get moving, people."

The air mage at her side nodded, lifting her hands and

sending the message down the line. The golden symbol for air, three straight lines across her chest, glistened in the evening light as the white arms of her tunic ruffled in the wind.

Aaliyah could hear the crowd even before they passed the sheared stone mountain that led into the capital. With the walls down, all of Titus waited for them, thousands of people, hundreds of thousands if she was honest with herself. Cheering. For her. Her stomach roiled even as she sat up straighter on Hassim, her beautiful horse. She pulled her spear tight to her chest and wished that they had taken more time on the road, enjoyed the slow journey back.

It wasn't that she didn't want to be home. She wanted her warm bed and her warmer woman. She wanted her people, and the people of the army she led, to have whatever or whoever they wanted as well. But she hated the fanfare her sister insisted upon—Odessa was all drama.

They took the curve and the smiling, yelling faces of the capital came into view. Despite the masses, she was grateful to finally glimpse the domes and obsidian spires of the palace Lockheart. As children, she and Odessa had always thought of it as their temple and now she called it home. She still couldn't stop the butterflies from dancing in her chest at the sight of it.

To Aaliyah's left, Sherrod, her third, was already smiling. He loved this part, and she was grateful that he did because someone should. Sherrod had spent much of their last down time re-pressing his hair, trying to tame his naturally soft curls to something even softer. He'd let one of his lovers dye it red a few days earlier, and Aaliyah had to admit the color suited his light brown skin. He ran a hand through his hair once more and Aaliyah rolled her eyes.

She looked to her right and caught Helima's eye. The other woman rolled her eyes but the rest of her face remained blank. Aaliyah could count on her second to agree that all this parading around was stupid. Helima's locs needed some attention but it would never have occurred to her to make sure they were done for this parade. Aaliyah cleared her throat and mimed a smile. The younger woman let her face relax into something just passable enough to be a smile.

Aaliyah sighed and returned her gaze to the people. She might not be happy to be on display but she was certainly happy to see them.The black and brown faces of the people of Titus blurred together for her as she did her best to smile and wave at them. The sound of her name on their lips was deafening. She tried to make eye contact with a few people as they went but found that nearly everyone lowered their gaze. It hadn't been that way two years ago, when she'd left to conquer the last of the southern realms for Odessa. She had seen their confidence in her, in the pledge that Odessa had made , and which Aaliyah had carried out. It troubled her, but maybe she wasn't the only one who didn't like the fanfare.

"Mistress Aaliyah! Mistress Aaliyah!" A chorus of tiny voices made Aaliyah stop her horse in front of four children along the edge of the crowd. Hassim went still as she balanced her spear and climbed down.

"General," Helima called out, but Aaliyah waved her away. "Don't come talking to me when your sister has you by the balls for being late."

The children's awed expressions made her smile. They stared at her black ceremonial armor, made of finely woven leather and coated in obsidian for strength and beauty. It shone in the afternoon light. Aaliyah could remember being their age and seeing the old king's guard wearing it, thinking how beautiful it was. How wonderful it would be to wear it.

Odessa had always been more interested in the crown.

"Wassup?" Aaliyah said, dropping down to her knees.

"You got food?" The littlest one asked, a boy no one more than four. His nappy curls looked uncombed and unwashed enough that Aaliyah surveyed the other three. Too thin. Their clothes threadbare.

She remembered that too.

Aaliyah stood up and turned back to Hassim. She gathered what remained of her rations from her case, then went to Sherrod and took his. Helima had already climbed down and carried hers over to the children. Together, they handed off the food, the kids' faces lit up like fire in the night. The littlest one hugged Aaliyah round the knees. She closed her eyes but she couldn't stop the tears from welling. She'd been a child who was this hungry, praying for someone to be kind.

Odessa had promised to be kind to the people of Titus when she became Queen.

Aaliyah mounted Hassim and waited patiently for Helima to climb back on her own mount. It took all of her strength to remain calm while she was seething. Odessa had better have answers for why there were hungry children on their streets.

TWO

Like the walls of the city, the gate of the palace dissolved into the ground, the stone rumbling and shifting, revealing the glory of Lockheart. The building gleamed in the waning light, fully revealing the domes of the great palace. The spires stood hundreds of men tall, each one twisted to catch the wind. Once each of the great elements had been visible in each tower's design: Air, Fire, Stone, Iron, Bone, and Water. The Queen had removed the sigils of iron and bone, the two mage orders that had stood with the old king. Though she understood Odessa's desire to show her strength and to warn others from rising against her, it still hurt Aaliyah's heart to not to see the carved bone statues in the first small courtyard, the pale white tile on the ground that was made from bone chips and the steel pikes and sculptures that had caught the light in the second. Ever since they'd been replaced with more stone and polished obsidian, the magical balance of the palace had always felt off.

Aaliyah climbed off Hassim and handed him over to the groom with a little kiss to his head. Sherrod and Helima left their mounts and the army behind in the third courtyard, the one dedicated to water. Lush greens filled the courtyard and two large ponds flanked the blue tiled walkway. Constant chimes showed the arrival of the wind as they walked through the air yard, the lightest of the rooms, the tile translucent. Beyond that, in the fire courtyard, flames danced across the dirt floors as they walked the red tiles. Sherrod made the flames part for them as they moved through. The last elemental courtyard was stone, untiled, where one long slab of stone moved gently beneath their feet.

The final courtyard, the true entrance to the palace, was traditionally decorated in the style of the current ruler. When Aaliyah had last seen it, it had held stone statues and a few small pieces of finery here and there.

Now the trees and statues dripped with gold, not mere gold paint but gold necklaces, chains, and even some jewels. The receiving group at the palace glittered just as much as the decor. They wore Odessa's signature gold, but they too were more opulent than simply color. Gold chains dripped from the necks of the assemblage, gold bracelets and rings adorned their arms and hands. Aaliyah could see from the curves of their bodies that they were well-fed.

Aaliyah gritted her teeth at the finery: here was gold for the people, here was food for their empty bellies. She returned her attention to the palace doors which, as if on cue, opened.

The sight of Odessa tamped some of Aaliyah's anger down. Her Queen glimmered in the sunlight, the gown she wore showing off every curve in her figure and drawing Aaliyah's thoughts to the soft unexposed skin. Her full mouth was painted red and her high cheekbones glittered, as though they had been dusted in gold. Odessa's hair had been worked into tiny braids and pulled up off her long neck. It had been two years since Aaliyah's tongue had traversed the path of that neck. Aaliyah guarded her features, not wanting anyone to see the desire there. There must have been some who knew but it was important, Odessa always said, to keep their relationship quiet. Not everyone would understand. Not everyone would care that they did not share blood; after all, they had been raised as sisters.

Kings married cousins but this was different.

Odessa descended into the courtyard slowly and deliberately. Everyone dropped to one knee as the Queen made her way past them. Her courtiers had changed so much from their early days.

Once, Odessa had kept warriors at her side. Aaliyah had known those people well. Now though, only the most beautiful and the richest kneeled around them. Yes, she recognized a few faces, but those were merchants, people who could move money and product.

Aaliyah was transfixed by her sister's beauty. She held Odessa's dark eyed stare. Odessa stopped a few feet from Aaliyah and waited, her perfectly manicured eyebrow going up. Aaliyah dropped to one knee.

Odessa's hand lifted and stone gates rose from beneath the ground, sealing them inside the inner walls. Aaliyah took a deep breath. Aaliyah didn't have even a hint of magical power in her. *Spiritless*, they called it, the formal term. *Magli*, the kids on the street had always called her.

"My champion." Odessa held out her hand, her voice husky and quiet.

"My Queen." Aaliyah took the offered hand and kissed it.

Odessa pressed her hand to Aaliyah's cheek. Aaliyah turned into the touch. Odessa's magic coursed through Aaliyah's stone armor, lapping at her skin, invisibly caressing her. The armor flexed and released, cupping her as tightly as her sister's hands. Aliyah fought the moan that threatened to burst forth. She might not have her sister's magic, but she did have her eye.

Odessa lifted Aaliyah's chin so that they could look at each other, the smile on her full lips smug. "You have returned home to me. Let us feast in your honor."

Aaliyah 's anger returned in a surge of heat.

Odessa cocked her head, studying her sister's face. "Speak warrior, if you have something to say."

"You honor me, my Queen. Will you honor me further and give my feast to the people of the capital?"

Aaliyah noted the slight flare in her sister's nostrils, the long intake of breath as she considered her next words. Aaliyah's skin again flared hot with magic, but this time it pricked and twisted over her skin, like Odessa's nails had done when she was angry as a child. The obsidian in Aaliyah's uniform tightened, forcing her to take a quick out breath.

She wondered if anyone who looked at them would still see

two sisters, happy to be reunited.

Odessa released Aaliyah's chin slowly. Her hands came to rest at her sides and Aaliyah watched her clench her fingers to keep from lashing out.

"If that is your wish," Odessa said. "Will you and your people not eat?"

"My people will eat with your people."

"Good. Then you and I will go without."

Odessa snapped her fingers and a few of her attendants rushed back inside the Palace. Aaliyah turned to Helima, but her second was already nodding. She would make sure their people were fed.

"Will you provide me with an update on the campaign, General?" Odessa said. She didn't wait for an answer, she turned on her heels and strode into the palace.

Aaliyah stood and she could feel every eye in the courtyard on her. She turned to Sherrod and Helima. "You'll take care of everything?"

"I got you, General," Helima said. "Take care of yourself."

Aaliyah tried to stand a little straighter. She was a warrior, a champion for the people. She was not still afraid of her big sister. Aaliyah took a deep breath and strode into the palace.

THREE

When they'd been children, Odessa's temper tantrums had always scared her. Rocks would often fly across the yard in front of the brothel, and once the future Queen had even managed to pull down a piece of the wall. But when she'd been frightened, Odessa had always soothed her, always promised she would keep her safe. Aaliyah's mother had never believed it. Had always tried to remind her of the fear.

Perhaps her inability to shake Aaliyah's faith had spurred her mother's leaving as much as any fear she might have felt.

Aaliyah stalked into her chamber trying to be as confident as her younger self. She was the Champion of the realm. Odessa would never hurt her, not really.

The room had been aired, the bedding changed, and a large copper tub had been placed in the center of the room. Candles had been placed around the room, unlit, and it looked like Odessa had planned a romantic evening. There were no fallen stones now, no rocks to fly at Aaliyah's face. Guilt welled in her stomach like oil, thick and heavy.

Odessa stared out the window, unmoving. Aaliyah gently closed the door behind her, locking it, and made her way to the copper tub. The tub yet held a little bit of water, no doubt the plan had been to fill it while they enjoyed the evening meal.

Aaliyah tapped the rim of the tub. "I feel like an ain't shit magli right now."

"That's because you ain't shit."

"I should have handled that differently."

Odessa turned to look at her, her make up streaked with tears. Aaliyah closed the distance between them and pulled Odessa into her arms. The Queen sobbed and Aaliyah held her tighter.

"How could you do that in front of everyone? As though I'd done something wrong? I'm here trying to make this kingdom work and you're off playing with your spear—"

"There is nothing fun about watching people die," Aaliyah said. Odessa pulled away.

"You have no idea what this is like. You *know* how to be a warrior, but I'm *learning* to be a Queen. And here you come criticizing me like I'm a child, in front of all my friends. All *our* allies. All those people whose influence I *need* to keep this kingdom running. If I'd done that to you—"

"I'm sorry!" Aaliyah closed her eyes, trying to suppress some of her anger.

Odessa wasn't wrong. Neither of them had been trained to rule. They'd believed that they could run it better than the man they'd merc'd, but they didn't know *how* to do it. They'd been nineteen and twenty when Odessa was crowned and five years was hardly long enough to learn the ins and outs of ruling. Aaliyah had been training to fight since she was five. Odessa had always used her mind and her magic, but problems that relied on blood were Aaliyah's. But ruling was a different beast.

"You're right. Of course you're right. I should have talked to you about it privately. Tried to understand you. Instead, I've ruined our first evening together in two years."

"Because you ain't shit," Odessa whispered, wiping her face. Aaliyah pulled Odessa back again.

"How bout if I call for someone to finish filling the tub, light all these candles and we get you naked? How does that sound?"

Odessa bit her lip, fighting a smile. "That sounds alright."

"Good."

Aaliyah kissed the top of Odessa's hair, squeezing her tight. Odessa looked up at her. Aaliyah dipped her head and Odessa pressed up on her toes until their mouths met. Aaliyah moaned. She'd waited so long to be here with her woman, in their home. What did it matter who heard them? She could pretend that nothing was wrong for just one night.

FOUR

One night became two, and two became three, and suddenly Aaliyah'd been home a week and only left her room once, to lay in the garden and let the sun beat down on her black skin. Odessa stayed damn near glued to her side, but she did manage to disappear in the early mornings to accomplish some sort of work.

After a week, though, Aaliyah could not be confined. She was a general and a woman of action. She couldn't just sit on her ass. Before she went out, she dressed for rest, replacing her uniform for simple white tunic and black pants—she didn't want anyone thinking she was on official business during her little outing. She smiled at every person she met as she moved through the Palace, chatting with those she knew and introducing herself to those she didn't.

When she reached the clerk's office there was no one inside. She closed the door gently behind her. Shelves of ledgers and journals lined the walls and stood in the center of the circular room. Some of the books had neatly printed titles and dates, others appeared to be cobbled together from sheets of paper and pressed into a folio. Aaliyah had no idea where to start and limited time to figure it out.

An open ledger rested on a low shelf near one of the great

windows. Aaliyah meandered over to see what it was. The ledger contained a list in Jalil's perfect handwriting. She'd missed her old friend. Jalil had been a voice of reason when they'd taken down the king. He was magli like her, and like her he made up for it with other talents. She ran her fingers over his careful scrawl:

Sutton Builders: 4,000 pieces
Mardell Linens and Co.: 9,000 pieces
Camfar and Sons: 2,000 pieces

Aaliyah studied the list but couldn't be sure what they accounted for. No doubt Jalil would know but then she'd have to wait for him and then she might have to try to explain. She'd rather noto take Jalil into her confidence. She would leave that to Helima.

Aaliyah chose the shelf that the open ledger rested as her starting place, hoping that the clerks preferred to have the newer ledgers closest to them. She made a gross miscalculation which she only realized after skimming through three ledgers that were not labeled. She tried the opposite tack, going for the furthest shelf, but there she was thwarted too. She was about to just turn in a circle and point when Jalil returned to his office.

He was as scrawny as ever, five feet five inches and a hundred pounds soaking wet. His hormones seemed to be suiting him, as he'd grown a beard since she'd last seen him. His brown face went from complete shock to amusement as he surveyed the places she'd been rummaging.

"Welcome home, General," Jalil said.

Aaliyah rolled her eyes and crossed the room to him. Helima had added Jalil to their crew when they were sixteen and he'd made a good ally for strategy with Odessa. He had a head for details and an education, was it any wonder that Odessa had put him in the clerk's office? They dapped and she pulled him in for a big hug. He smelled like hair oil and coffee.

"You look good, old man," she said. Jalil ducked his head, returning to the makeshift desk. "Have you seen Helima yet?"

Jalil paused. "No. I thought maybe you had kept her busy."

"Oh, she might be doing inventory," Aaliyah lied. "Doesn't want to see you until the numbers are right."

Jalil nodded but he didn't look at her. He knew what she looked like when she lied. He wanted to believe her.

"In other news J, I need your help."

He turned to look at her now, leaning against the back of his chair and trying to force a bigger smile on his face. "Don't you always? What do you need?"

"I'm looking for the ledger from last summer. We ordered additional cannons for the front but only received one of the five we requested. Do you have the procurement order?"

Jalil moved to a shelf in the middle of the room. Aaliyah snorted. It was the last place she would have looked.

"August, right?" Jalil said. "We had a lot of spending then, so it spans two books."

"A lot of spending? Why? I didn't think we requested that much," Aaliyah said.

Jalil didn't take the bait, he returned to the desk, sat and opened one of the ledgers. "It's just that way sometimes."

Aaliyah waited patiently while he looked through one ledger and then the other. He scowled at the lists before finally stopping on one line. He handed the book to Aaliyah.

Solar Blacksmith: 2,000 pieces
Mardell Linens and Co.: 15,000 pieces

Aaliyah swallowed. "The blacksmith is our canon?"

"Yes."

"We only purchased one canon?"

"Yes," Jalil said tentatively.

"And Mardell Linens is?"

Jalil wouldn't meet her eyes. "The Queen's dressmaker."

Aaliyah bit back a curse. "How many gowns does fifteen thousand pieces buy?"

"Five."

"All for the queen?" Aaliyah looked up into Jalil's face. He looked down at his feet and bit his lip as though willing himself silent. She waited until she reined in enough of the anger throbbing in her chest to speak calmly. "Thank you, Jalil, this has been helpful. I'll make sure Helima brings you the inventory."

Aaliyah handed him the book back and turned to go. He grabbed her arm. "Be careful."

She smiled. "Why? I'm not doing anything."

Jalil nodded and quickly turned away from her. He didn't believe a word she'd said.

FIVE

Aaliyah found Helima was sitting on her bunk with a book in her hand when she entered the barracks. Sherrod was out like a light. Aaliyah whistled and both of her people followed her back out of the barracks into the afternoon sun. Sherrod only required one kick from Helima. Aaliyah led them to a tree in the far corner of the training yard where they could be afforded some privacy.

Before them stood new recruits learning the careful formations of the army: scrawny and fat, every gender and lack thereof. They practiced their first formation—it involved raising their spears up to their full height and then down into an army-rending strike.

"Out of your sex haze, huh?" Sherrod said. "If I were you I'd still be in bed right now. And when exactly are you going to mention the name of your pretty maid to me? I just think we should know if we're sharing—"

Aaliyah shot him a look.

"I'll be quiet now," he said quickly, looking down at his feet and then out at the yard.

Helima said nothing, studying Aaliyah's face. Aaliyah took a deep breath, pushing her anger down as much as she could.

"You haven't seen Jalil," she said.

Helima looked at the ground. "That's your business?"

"It hurts him," Aaliyah said. "And that's my business."

Helima sighed and crossed her arms. Sherrod looked between them. For all that he was her third he still didn't entirely understand their relationship, he wasn't yet privy to their secrets. She liked Sherrod, and appreciated that he was gifted in fire, but he didn't have their bond. He didn't understand the loyalty of the street. Aaliyah had fed Helima one night when she'd been young and hungry, and the younger woman had followed her ever since. Odessa had thought it was funny but Aaliyah had always understood the gift that Helima's trust was.

"I'll see him," Helima said.

"And talk to him," Aaliyah added. Helima rolled her eyes but she nodded. "I need to know what's been happening here while we've been gone."

Helima's eyes narrowed. She *should* know that it wasn't just about that. Aaliyah wanted to know about what had been happening but she had other sources. She held Helima's gaze.

"Sherrod?"

"Yes, ma'am?"

She sucked her teeth.

"Damn, I can't do nothing right today," Sherrod said.

"You have a maid you can ask don't you? About what's been going on?"

"Yeah. Ashanti'll tell me."

Helima sighed and nodded her head slightly. Good, Aaliyah needed her to understand.

"What are you going to do?" Helima asked.

"I'm going to the 'Ville."

"Odessa will throw a fit," Helima said.

"Not to mention you'll get robbed," Sherrod added. Aaliyah and Helima both snorted. "Fuck you guys. Just cause you're a couple of bad asses from a fucked up—"

"Magli, I'll be fine. But you don't go down there," Aaliyah said. She looked back at Helima. "I need Mercedes' point of view. She won't lie to my face."

"Damn," Sherrod said.

"She means from who was left behind. She trusts you fine,"

Helima said, rolling her eyes. "Sensitive ass. We'll do the palace work. Just be careful around that bitch."

Aaliyah nodded, warmed by the exchange. For all that she pretended to be a hard ass, Helima was a big softie. Now she just had to get out of the palace without Odessa noticing.

SIX

It took a few hours to contrive a plan to get out of the Palace. She put together an outfit from old clothes, things that barely fit her now, since she'd built more muscle on the road. No one would think she was a general in the plain grey tunic and even darker grey pants. She collected them into a tight bundle and took them down toward the kitchen, like they were laundry.

"General?" A small voice said.

Aaliyah cursed her misfortune. The child before her smiled, their bright white skin turning pink. They did not have the look of the Oxnar people, who were a similar milky white but with features that tended more sharp and severe, so Aaliyah recognized them for what they were, *stripped* as they said on the street, their flesh washed away of brown by the many gods. They looked down at their feet then up at Aaliyah again.

"How may I help you, little one?" Aaliyah asked. The child pinked further, the flush spreading to their neck.

"I...if...if it pleases you, I could take your laundry," they said and Aaliyah looked down at the bundle.

She looked back up at the child ,catching a glimpse of a figure in the mouth of another hallway ahead of them. She'd seen the flap of black cloth as they ducked back into the shadows. She glanced over her shoulder but saw no one at her back, only the marbled hall she'd already traversed. Aaliyah felt anger rise in her.Someone was watching her. In the Palace. Who would dare? The child sucked in a breath and Aaliyah refocused, smoothing her features so she didn't look so upset.

"Thank you for the offer. Would you mind very much if I walked with you?" Aaliyah asked.

The child's eyes bulged and a hand went up to their short cropped hair before they brought it back to their side, an aborted self-soothing gesture. Aaliyah hazarded a glance at the shadows but could see nothing there now.

"If...if it pleases you," the child said.

Aaliyah nodded, standing up straight and holding out her hand. The child blinked rapidly, then tucked their hand into Aaliyah's. Their fingers were clammy with nerves but Aaliyah squeezed them reassuringly before turning them back on their path.

The child didn't chatter, simply led and Aaliyah appreciated the silence. She could hear, now that she knew to listen, the slight sound of swishing fabric behind them. They'd used air magic to quiet themselves, but not completely. Whoever wanted her followed must be counting on her magli ass not to notice, or didn't care that they might be found out.

"Why are you bringing down your own laundry?" the child asked, breaking through her thoughts.

"I didn't want to be in my room. What's your name?"

"Ko."

"How long have you worked in the palace, Ko?"

"All my life," they said.

Aaliyah nodded. The child had to be at least nine, long enough then to have experienced the old king, who preferred to keep his servants, more like slaves, close.

"I grew up in the 'Ville," Aaliyah said. Ko sucked in a breath and unconsciously squeezed her fingers. She knew what people thought of her home district: that it was full of nobody but thieves, whores and addicts. The source of cassa adu, the drug that ravaged Titus and felt like the greatest love those who smoked it could ever know. They weren't wrong but it was also more than that. "It's not so bad, little one, but it means I don't do well with being indoors so long. I like to lean against walls outside."

Ko nodded, their expression grave. They looked as if they might speak, but hesitated, peering about as if someone might overhear them. Aaliyah took the moment to look back over her shoulder but she still couldn't see who was following them. Ko leaned in and Aaliyah bent her knees so the child could whisper in her ear.

"I know a secret place where you can be outside but within the walls."

Aaliyah cocked an eyebrow. "Where is that?"

Ko smiled and then took Aaliyah's hand again, pulling her as quickly as their little legs would carry. Before long they were running, drawing the attention of other servants. Aaliyah tried to slow them, to allow her to plan how to best shake their shadow but Ko's running seemed to have it covered. Their shadow had disappeared. She noticed that somehow they had lost their shadow.

Ko took a few turns that left Aaliyah dizzy—she didn't know the palace well enough yet—before arriving at a door that Ko flung open and released them into a garden.

Aaliyah had never seen its like. Instead of traditional trees, each of the long limbs and rotund trunks were stark white, with leaves that looked more like straightened hair blowing in the wind. The flowers were also porcelain but their petals were green, blue, gray and brown, the colors of eyes. Nothing was overgrown, the brown bushes trimmed neatly against the grand stone wall. Someone had been tending this garden.

Aaliyah released Ko's hand, turning in circles. "What garden is this?"

"The garden of bone," Ko said, their smile brilliant. "If you follow the path, it leads you out to the main road, through the side of a great wall."

"I didn't know that."

"No one does. Everyone who knew it is dead."

Aaliyah stopped and looked at them, wondering just how much death they had seen in their young years. She started to ask them but then thought better of it, they didn't need to rehash all the ways that Ko had been traumatized. The child was giving her a gift, she could repay it without pain.

"This is beautiful. Thank you for sharing it with me."

"You're welcome."

They led Aaliyah back through the hallway at a slower pace and she committed the route to memory. She let Ko lead her to the laundry and pretended to leave her items. She kissed the child on the cheek, which turned their pale face beet red, before they kissed her cheek too and took off running.

Aaliyah retrieved her bundle with little effort and made her way back to the garden of bone.

SEVEN

Ko hadn't lied, the little bone strewn path led to a great wall with an ancient door of petrified wood. Aaliyah changed and hid her clothes behind a shrub. When she exited the garden, she ended up in the palace commons, the district nearest the palace walls, the grandeur of the houses showing that they at least were not suffering under Odessa. The commons was marked by its wealth but also by the ornate stone decorations which only the palace commons residents could afford to create to honor the magic of their ruler. Aaliyah wondered briefly how no one in the palace had known about it, only a magli former slave and now the General of the great army. She decided not to judge her gift but to accept it and praise the gods later.

She made her way through the city unnoticed but not without taking stock of her city. The beautiful, dark stone houses of palace commons were nearly as tall as the palace walls and cleaned daily by some servant or another. Here lived merchants and those not quite rich or important enough to have apartments within the palace walls. Aaliyah lowered her head as she moved through the area, though the streets were traveled mainly by servants, the masters who might know her face inside or still drunk from the night before.

When Aaliyah left palace commons and passed through the

neighborhoods of Echo and Oxi, she began to see the sorts of conditions she had expected to change.

When Odessa had become queen, she'd promised Aaliyah that she'd build homes for the homeless, keep people fed, find ways to keep children safe and off the streets. Yet here Aaliyah was five years later, surrounded by people sleeping on the cobblestones, hungry and sick. She saw a few people with eyes burned out and white, their flesh falling from their bones—adu withdrawal. They reminded her of her mother, before she'd disappeared. Aaliyah wondered if she would find the woman now among the addicts, could envision Odessa's wicked smile if she did. Odessa was meant to be helping and yet the people suffered. Perhaps even worse than they had under the old king.

Whistles and chirps sounded from the rooftops as she crossed into the 'Ville. The kids playing lookout scurried off and the corner boys disappeared into mud brick buildings. She cocked her head and listened. The sounds of the 'Ville brought a smile to her lips. They were the same chirps and rhythms that she grew up with. They hadn't tagged her as military, at least not yet. A boy of no more than sixteen, well fed and well dressed in his leather pants and shoes, fell into step with her. They walked for a full block before she acknowledged him with a nod. He sped up and turned so he could keep one eye on her face and the other on the path ahead of them.

"Wassup? Whachu need?"

"Nothing you got," Aaliyah said. She was waiting for bigger prey.

"I got everything. Everything a pretty thing like you could need."

Aaliyah snorted. She knew she wasn't the boy's type. She wore her hair in knots across her head, bound her chest flat and accentuated her muscle. Boys like him wanted a trophy to look pretty on their arm. Aaliyah was no one's trophy.

"I need Madame Mercy," Aaliyah said. "Unless you've got access to her you can't help me."

The boy stopped, let her get ahead of him and then followed. "Ain't nobody got access to Madame Mercy except Big Blue, and Big Blue don't give that shit up for nobody."

Aaliyah raised an eyebrow. "He still follows her like a puppy, huh?"

The boy snickered. "Hell yeah."

"He feed y'all?"

The boy stopped and Aaliyah did the same, letting him assess her. He spit into the dirt.

"You guard?"

Aaliyah sucked her teeth. "Used to sling too. Now I'm asking you about how well your boss keeps you in food and a roof. And you're going to answer because you don't want trouble with me."

He stepped up to her, bumping their chests together. "I ain't saying shit. I don't give a fuck about you."

She sighed. She'd hoped to avoid an altercation. Aaliyah pushed the boy back and he swung. Blue wasn't teaching boys how to fight anymore, that was for sure. She blocked his punch and swung back, landing her blow perfectly against the bridge of his nose. He grunted as the force knocked him back.

He spat again, this time with blood. "Feed me fine. Little brothers too. Ain't never met no guard who slang before. Who the hell—"

"You talk too much, boy," a gruff voice said behind them. They turned to look at the speaker.

Big Blue was as black as midnight on a moonless night. He was built like an ox and he used his bulk to intimidate just about everyone but the gutter cats of the neighborhood. One curled around his tree trunk of a leg, purring. His dark eyes took Aaliyah in quickly and he grunted.

"Aaliyah."

"Blue."

"You ain't supposed to be here without an invitation," Blue said.

"I go where I please," she said.

Blue shook his head. "Same old, Aaliyah. Always looking for a slight."

The boy looked at him. "Wait. Aaliyah? *The* Aaliyah? The one who—"

"What I say about your mouth, boy?"

The boy's jaw snapped shut, his teeth clacking.

Blue returned his attention to her. "Whachu want?"

"I want to talk."

"You wanna start a war," Blue said.

"No, I don't."

"Your sister know you're here?" Aaliyah didn't answer and he nodded. "Yeah, it's a war you want, and Madame's too eager to give it to her. Come on."

Blue turned, crouching down to pet the cat one more time, and shot the boy a commanding look. "Back to your corner and keep your mouth shut, will you?"

"Yeah." The boy smiled brightly at Aaliyah. "I'm gonna tell everyone I met you."

Aaliyah could see the child beneath the bravado, excited to meet a war hero. Blue led them through the tangle that was the 'Ville. Once, Aaliyah could have pinpointed every drop house and brothel on the block, but now the places she'd known were run down or shuttered. She thought of asking Blue but said nothing for now. They reached a house that had once belonged to the Prince of Thieves, thick walled and tall for the area. The perfect vantage place to see his enemies.

Aaliyah remembered fondly the older man's great white smile, more like a blade then his actual knife. He'd taught Aaliyah dagger work, teaching her to strike his daughter into the dust, even as he taught Mercy to use bone magic to twist Aaliyah's limbs. Mercy had never minded, and Aaliyah had enjoyed the feel of Mercy's cool dry hands against her own. Enjoyed the feel of the bone magic as it stitched her back together. Their first kiss had been in the eaves of this house, their lips joining in the same way their hands did.

Mercy must be getting sentimental if she was staying here again.

Blue took her to the back entrance, through a kitchen where several young women sat trying to get warm by the fire. Aaliyah tried to ignore how young they were and focused instead on the fact that they looked fed and happy. They chatted to each other, whispering and laughing. Blue thundered up the back stairs and Aaliyah hurried to catch up with him.

A long hallway brought them to the room that the Prince of

Thieves had once used as his armory. Blue knocked and then they waited. Aaliyah's heart quickened. Blue knocked a second time. The door opened and there she was.

Mercedes barely reached Aaliyah's chin in her bare feet, but today she wore tall black boots that put her at eye level. Her knee-length hair hung free in a sea of twists. She wore a dress of black leather that accentuated the blessed bounty of her breasts and backside. Her hands were covered in blood and behind her someone writhed on the floor in agony..

Mercedes lips twisted into a smile."Hey babe, I'm just finishing some business. You want to come in or wait out there?"

Aaliyah looked from the man to Mercedes. "In."

Mercedes bit her lip. "I love it when you watch me."

Mercy stepped aside to let them into the room. She'd replaced the racks of spears, daggers and bows with a neat little office. A settee sat against the far wall in front of the hearth. A large desk sat against one wall with a chair behind it and across from it, The Prince of Thieves' prize spear and dagger hung. Mercy was definitely getting sentimental. Aaliyah circled the pool of blood and sat on the settee against the far wall. Mercy returned her attention to the man on the floor, hauling him up by the collar of his shirt. He was clean shaven and looked too young to be having the life beaten out of him. His once white shirt looked expensive. Either Mercy paid him well, or he was stealing. Blood gurgled from his full lips.. Aaliyah clamped her teeth shut. This was Mercy's place, her rules. She wouldn't interfere.

"Now see, I've spent too much time on you," Mercy said, shaking an agonized cry out of the man. "What do you think babe? Kill him or just cut his dick off?"

The man broke out into hysterical wailing and Mercy rolled her eyes. She let him slump back to the floor and sob into the wood. Mercy strode over to her desk, grabbing a cloth and wiping her hands.

"What's he done?" Aaliyah asked.

"He's a runner. A good runner. But he stole from me, beat one of my girls and refused to pay her. So really he stole from me twice."

"He's a good earner?"

Mercy shrugged.

"Why not just take his hand and let him get back to work?"

Mercy sauntered over to the settee. She settled herself in Aaliyah's lap. Aaliyah's eyes were drawn to her red lips. Mercy traced her hand down Aaliyah's arm, until she looked Aaliyah in the eyes.

"You're such a softie. You think everyone is as honest as you. But love, if I let him go, he's going to steal from me again. And stealing from me is stealing from my family." Mercy's eyes went from playful to stone. She lifted her hand and twisted, the grace of it undeniable. It shouldn't have surprised her, Mercy'd learned to make the brutality of bone magic look elegant on Aaliyah's own flesh. Aaliyah flinched at the sound of the man's neck breaking. Mercy stopped smiling and stood. "Blue, clean that up. Aaliyah, tell me what the fuck you're doing in my territory without permission."

Aaliyah preferred this Mercy, the tactical one. Yes, she was colder, but that meant Aaliyah didn't have to deal with the feelings she'd harbored since they were teens. Blue lifted the body of the dead man and went out without so much as a second glance. "You may know I've just returned home."

Mercy snorted. "I may know that. What's it got to do with me and mine?"

"When I came into the city, I noticed a few children who looked...under cared for."

"Only a few, she did a great job with the round up," Mercy muttered.

"Just now on my way here I saw a lot more than that. Hungry kids, sick folks. It looked worse than before I left. People looked worse." Aaliyah sighed. "I need to know what's been going on here. I need to know what she's been doing and I trust you to tell me."

For a moment, Aaliyah was sure Mercy would send her packing. Her nostrils flared and her eyes narrowed to ward off angry tears. She'd worn the same expression the day Odessa had told Aaliyah to choose and Aaliyah had placed her hand, and her faith, in Odessa's words. Mercy sat back on the edge of her desk.

"Nothing has been going on here. She closed every kitchen open to the hungry, every workhouse. All gone. The orphanage where your mother left you? Shuttered. The children on the street. The hospital, abandoned. Your sister did the opposite of everything she said she would do," Mercy said. "And this conversation is treason."

"What?"

"Criticism of the Queen shall be considered treason and all those found to be committing treason shall be beheaded," Mercy recited in a courtly tone. Aaliyah studied the floor. Why hadn't she known about this? Suddenly Jalil's warning made more sense. *Be careful*, he'd said. "I know you love her, babe, but she lied to us. People are scared and sick and hungry."

"Why would she do this?"

"What?"

"Any of it," Aaliyah said. "Why lie? Why take from the people? Why?"

"Power's always been Odessa's adu. You may not like it but she's been begging you for hits over the years and becoming queen is like the biggest one she'd ever had—"

"Enough," Aaliyah said. She closed her eyes shut to keep from crying. Mercy's shoes clacked on the floor as she made her way over. Aaliyah opened her eyes as Mercy moved her knees apart and knelt in between them.

"This isn't your fault," Mercy said.

"I made promises to people. That things would get better. She would be better," Aaliyah said. "But it's worse."

"Aali, that's not your fault. She's doing this. She's spent more on gowns and trips than her people. She made those choices, not you. You always manage to see the good in people. Even when there is no good in them," Mercy said.

"I don't want to have this argument with you," Aaliyah said.

"What argument?"

"There *is* good in her, Mercedes. She may not know how to deal with people the way you do but she has goodness in her. And she loves me." A cruel smile ghosted across Mercy's face before she turned her head.

"You're right, we're not having this argument."

"Where has she been going on trips?" Aaliyah said, tracking back.

"She took one long trip last year east to Galavera. And this year she went west to Oxnar."

Aaliyah's mind turned. Tactically, Galavera and Oxnar were the only countries with militaries strong enough to rival Titus, since Aaliyah herself had defeated every army to the south. Galavera and Oxnar made dangerous enemies but valuable potential allies.

"For what?"

Mercy considered her words and spoke carefully. "Both Kings are unmarried. Rumor has it she's courting them."

Aaliyah blinked."I told her she should try to make Galavera and Oxnar allies but…"

"What better way than by making one of them her husband?" Mercy took her hands but Aaliyah pulled away, getting up so she could lean against the wall.

Aaliyah loved Odessa more than anything. She had killed a king for her. Odessa had always promised that they would have each other. She'd alway said that *nothing* would change that.

Aaliyah was so angry she couldn't see straight.

"Rumor has it one of them is interested." Mercy wrapped her arms around Aaliyah's waist. "There are some people who are considering a show of resistance. People who think the only true Queen is the one we all call champion."

Aaliyah spun around but Mercy didn't release her, just held the other woman tight against her.

"Who?" Aaliyah said.

"You. You could be Queen."

"I'm a soldier."

"You're a champion. A leader who will focus on the needs of your people."

"Mercy, *this* is treason."

"What's one more charge?" Mercy's brown eyes searched Aaliyah's face. "You could do it. I know you could."

"Odessa is the Queen. I am her sword," Aaliyah said.

Mercy released her, stepping backward. Aaliyah saw the expression on her face go hard again. "Gods forbid you should be your own sword."

They stared at each other. Mercy was all heat, the anger and disappointment radiating off of her in waves. Aaliyah was cool, her breath coming with difficulty. She tried not to think of that moment when she'd walked away with Odessa. When the Prince of Thieves had taken his protection away after so many years. She was overwhelmed and Mercy knew it. If she hadn't, she would have kept pushing. Like they were fifteen again and Mercy was pressing Aaliyah to think of someone other than Odessa. To put her own needs first. She'd pushed and pushed and Aaliyah had run off. Disappearing to the woods for two weeks. When she'd returned, Mercy hadn't pushed her again, knew not to push Aaliyah harder than she could take.

"I think we're done for the day. You come back when you're ready for more," Mercy said, turning away.

Aaliyah's eyes caught the pool of blood that was still in the middle of Mercy's floor. She could see her own reflection in it.

Aaliyah had always accepted that she would bear the stain of the blood she'd shed for her sister, because Odessa would do what was right. Now she didn't know if she could.

EIGHT

Aaliyah was exhausted and hungry by the time she returned to the palace. She took Ko's secret route, grateful not to have to answer questions when she reached the gate. She stopped for no one as she made her way to her chamber. She wanted nothing more than to crawl in her bed and think of nothing.

There were stones strewn across the floor in front of her doorway, making Aaliyah pause. She felt like a child again, nervous about what Odessa might do. Her hand shook as she turned the door knob.

She wasn't surprised to find Odessa lying across her bed when she entered the room, but her stomach still lurched. Aaliyah went straight into her dressing room without acknowledging her.

She washed herself and put on her bed clothes before returning to the chamber. Odessa hadn't moved but Aaliyah could feel power sparking in the room. Her sister was angry too.

"Good evening," Aaliyah said. She crossed the room, blowing out candles as she went.

"Good evening, General Aaliyah. So kind of you to join us," Odessa said.

"I'm not in the mood," Aaliyah said.

"Why? Didn't your little girl in the 'Ville make you feel good?" Odessa said.

Aaliyah stopped. She looked at her sister, tried to read her intent. Odessa's eyes were wide and frantic. Aaliyah stood up a little straighter. She was fishing.

"I went for a walk. I didn't like what I saw, but I'm willing to discuss it with you in a reasonable manner. Just not right now."

"As your Queen I have every right to know what you've been doing with your time."

Aaliyah nodded. "You're right. I went to Samza Orphanage."

She watched Odessa's face, looking for a reaction. It was the orphanage that Aaliyah's mother had deposited them at before she'd wandered off to safety and her adu. Odessa raised a manicured eyebrow but there was nothing remorseful or guilty in her expression.

"Why would you go to that place?"

Aaliyah shrugged. "Wanted to see the old place. Did you know it closed?"

Odessa laughed. "Enough of this bullshit about Samza. You hated that place and it was decrepit when we were there. You want me to believe you didn't go see your whore?"

"I don't want you to believe anything. I want you to get out of my room. I want to go to sleep, so that tomorrow we can have a productive conversation," Aaliyah said.

"Don't play games with me," Odessa snapped.

Aaliyah stood over the bed. "I'm not playing games. Good night, Odessa."

Odessa looked ready to burst with anger. The walls cracked and heaved with the tension of her power. Aaliyah waited, steeling herself. She wished she had her sword.

Odessa climbed out of the bed, knocking into Aaliyah's shoulder. She stomped across the room, her chest heaving with unexpressed anger. She opened the door and turned back.

"One of these days, Aaliyah, you are going to regret forgetting where your loyalties lie. Good night, sister mine." She slammed the door shut behind her.

Aaliyah shook as she climbed into bed, the only light in the room the glow from the fireplace. Everything Mercy had said was true. Odessa was up to no good. There was nothing she could do except try to change that.

NINE

Aaliyah's sleep was restless. She dreamed of her mother, a woman she hadn't seen since she was three years old. In the dream, her mother tried to keep Odessa away from her but Aaliyah just kept fighting and fighting and fighting to get to her sister. Eventually, her mother let her go and just disappeared. Always leaving them alone.

Aaliyah made her way down to the barracks. She needed an update from Sherrod and Helima, but she also needed to get back to her routine. She was a general after all, and her people deserved her attention. She tried to smile and make small talk as she moved through the castle, but either her face showed more than she wanted or everyone was simply busy, but no one seemed to want to talk to her.

It was so early that when she entered the barracks, most of the soldiers were still laying abed. The few awake waved to her and she waved back. Aaliyah checked first Helima's and then Sherrod's bunks. Both were empty.

"She's with Jalil," a quiet voice said. Aaliyah found a young private staring down at her, her hair dusty red and her eyes a mystifying green against her brown skin. "Not sure where he is. Probably with one of the maids."

"Thanks. When you see either of them will you let them know

I'm looking for 'em?" Aaliyah said.

The young woman nodded.

"Get your rest, private."

Aaliyah walked out of the barracks into the training yard and stopped short. Two mages, of stone and air as indicated by their tunics, strode towards her with grim expressions. The air mage wore turquoise ceremonial robes that skimmed the ground. Feather earrings dangled against her cheek and her hair was pulled back into a poof on the top of her head. Her companion was a big man with an unsettling smirk. His jagged teeth looked razor sharp. Aaliyah took a half step back. The private came up beside her, looking at the mages as well.

"Back to bed, private."

"I apologize for the disobedience, General, but I'll stay right here," the private said.

"General." The air mage stopped in front of them.

"Mage," Aaliyah said, steel in her voice. Other soldiers streamed out of the barracks at her back. The two mages surveyed the growing crowd and the air mage looked nervous. She cleared her throat.

"We are under strict orders from the Queen herself to escort you to the dungeon," the mage said.

Every soldier on the grounds went completely silent. Aaliyah tilted her head slightly, regarding the mage with interest. No one needed to know that her hands were shaking. That she could barely breathe.

"On what charge?" Aaliyah said, as if she were only curious.

"Treason," said the other mage. His smile gleamed with malice. She reckoned he expected to make his career off of her.

Any reply from her was lost in the soldiers' uproar. They wouldn't hear anything of it. The mages were liars, they yelled. The Queen would never. Aaliyah raised her hand and her people went silent.

"I'm sure this is a mistake. But I have no desire for bloodshed. Let's go for a walk," she said loud enough for her people to hear and then spoke more quietly to the private from earlier. "Find Helima."

"Yes, General." The private took off at a brisk run towards

the palace.

Aaliyah turned to the mages. "Shall we go?"

She strode forward, between the two mages. It took a moment but they followed her, allowing her to lead herself to the dungeons of Titus. She had never used them, and couldn't say whether Odessa had, but she'd heard the stories about the old king. The dungeons of Titus were where people went to suffer.. The King had enjoyed their pain. He'd been fond of hot irons.

Aaliyah prayed she looked strong as she passed servants and soldiers. Everyone she passed seemed to go quiet, watching her procession without objection. Had they known what Odessa planned? No one had warned her. How many friends had she lost to Odessa in the two years she'd been gone?

By the time she reached the dungeons, Aaliyah was seething. Odessa must have done this on purpose. She wanted to humiliate her in front of her people, to remind them who had the power. And she'd succeeded.

The mage with the aspirations slipped ahead of her and opened a stone cell, using magic to drop stone spires into the ground. When she'd become queen, Odessa had removed all the iron, because her gifts were with stone and she wanted nothing around that she couldn't manipulate. At the time Aaliyah had thought it wise. Now she wished she'd disagreed.

The mage raised five stone bars to the height of the room using his own magic to seal it. He smiled at her.

"Not so great are you? " he said. "Remember it was Rakheem who locked you away this day, General."

He spat on the floor of her cell. The other mage took his arm and led him away.

Aaliyah sat down on the stone bench inside the cell. She walked the full space of the cell like a caged animal, the heat draining from her body as her breath left her. What could she do from this cell?

A commotion started up the corridor. Aaliyah stood, pressing her face against the stone bars. She caught Helima shoving the butt of her knife into the Rakheem's gut. The ground rocked beneath their feet as he created a stone shield. Helima attempted to get around it, rolling to one side but the mage was too quick.

He retracted it as quickly as he'd produced it.

"Helima!" Aaliyah shouted. "Don't hurt them."

Rakheem turned his head to look at Aaliyah and Helima used it to her advantage, punching him so hard that he crumpled into a ball.. Helima tripped over him as she rushed to press herself against the pillars. Her face was twisted with anger, her clothes disheveled from fighting. The female mage was at her back, tentatively holding a bloody nose.

"I'm getting you out of here," Helima snarled.

"You're not," Aaliyah said

"She ca—"

"Don't. Get me mercy with words, not violence," Aaliyah said. She grabbed Helima's hands through the bars. "Get me mercy, Helima. That's what I need."

Helima took a deep breath and nodded. Aaliyah's second turned away abruptly, making the mage jump back before she followed Helima out of the dungeon. Rakheem followed a moment later, sparing a venomous glance at Aaliyah. All she could do was hope that Mercy would be enough.

TEN

Hours later, Aaliyah heard the sounds of someone headed towards her cell. She stood up and wished she hadn't. She felt dizzy, hunger like she'd only felt in her childhood, and her mouth was gummy with dehydration. She leaned against the pillars, hopeful that Helima was returning with Mercy.

Odessa shone radiant as the sun, her gown shimmering with its own light in the dark dungeon. She wore a crown of gold, twisted and braided in an infinite loop. She sauntered through the dungeon until she stood in front of Aaliyah, studying her face. Aaliyah waited. Whatever the Queen wanted, she would have to say it herself.

"You put me in an awkward position, Aaliyah. You questioned my actions in front of others—"

"And you forgave me. Or were all those hours on my knees not penance enough?" Aaliyah said. Odessa's nostrils flared. "Forgive me. I interrupted."

"You deliberately disobeyed me," Odessa said. "I told you I didn't want you anywhere near that woman."

"Mercy is one of our oldest friends—"

"Was one of our oldest friends. Was. But she has been spreading lies—"

"And what I saw with my own eyes?" Aaliyah said, righting

herself. Odessa went still. "Children unfed. The ill and infirm on the street. We made a promise—"

"*You* made a promise," Odessa said quietly. "We were children, Aali, we thought we understood what it meant to hold power. What it meant to keep it. We were wrong. Some have to suffer so that others can be well. We can't all be equal. You haven't been here to see what happens when you try to disrupt the order of things. People threatened my life, Aali. The only way to show them was to use my power. To make them see that they must fall in line behind me. So yes, you made promises. But the only promise I made was to keep you safe. And you're safest in this cell."

Aaliyah stared at the woman she loved, the woman she had given her entire life for. How could Odessa be so cruel? She didn't understand why this was supposed to be safe. There was shuffling of feet along the corridor and then Sherrod stood beside Odessa. He looked disheveled, like he'd been dragged out of bed. She hoped that meant he hadn't known. His eyes were big and round as he surveyed first Aaliyah and then the Queen. His face went blank and he slowly relaxed his eyes to match.

"My Queen, you sent for me?" Sherrod said.

"They tell me, Third Sherrod, that you are the next closest thing to a leader my army has, that you are a capable fire mage, that you are a leader who can be trusted. Is that so?" Odessa asked. Sherrod looked at Aaliyah and then back at Odessa.

"You'll forgive me my Queen, but the General's second is the closest thing to a leader your army has, assuming of course we are excluding the General," Sherrod said.

"Neither the General nor her second are equipped to lead my army at this time. That makes you next in line. Will you take the title of General?"

Sherrod looked at Aaliyah and she nodded, then he looked down at the ground. If he was smart he would take the job and keep their people safe. She couldn't begrudge him that.

"You honor me, my Queen," Sherrod said quietly. "But I cannot accept. No one will follow me. The General is your champion and the champion of the people."

Odessa sighed. "Lock him up."

"Odessa—" Aaliyah said. Odessa threw her hand up and the ground rushed to do her bidding, throwing Aaliyah back. The pillars expanded so that she couldn't see what was happening in the corridor. She could barely breath in the closed space. She could hear struggling and smell burning flesh, but nothing else. "Odessa!"

What she wouldn't give for an ounce of Odessa's power to keep this from happening. Aaliyah slammed herself into the stone and pain, electric and hot, shot through her shoulder. She didn't stop. She threw herself again and again, until the sounds outside stopped and the pain was too much. She slumped against the wall and let herself cry.

ELEVEN

The wall that led out of her cell began rumbling and rattling her teeth. Aaliyah opened her eyes to see what awaited her. It felt like she'd been locked in the dark for days. Ko stood in the doorway with a bowl and cup. They placed them on the floor at the mouth of the cell.

"What are you doing here, little one?" Aaliyah's voice was hoarse as she crouched down in front of the food. Her throat ached with dryness.

The bowl held grits smothered in butter with bits of bacon. Aaliyah took a bite and then sipped the cold water. She closed her eyes to savor it.

"Are you seeking mercy, General?" Ko said.

Aaliyah surveyed the child. They looked just as innocent as the day they'd shown her the bone garden. How much of that had been an act?

"What do you know about Mercy, Ko?"

"That she comes to those who are in need. In a minute, a guard will come. Your man will have to burn her."

"Ko—"

"Go through the corridor and down the steps. Someone will be waiting for you. "

"Ko—" she tried again.

"I'm sorry, General. She told me to tell you, she's sorry," Ko said softly.

Aaliyah nodded slowly. "I don't think you should call me General, Ko. The Queen stripped me of that title."

Ko's head cocked to one side. They raised a hand and the floor rumbled once more. Sherrod became visible as the cell door sunk into the ground.

"Aaliyah?" His eyes were unfocused.

Ko brought him his own bowl and some water.

"You'll only have a few minutes," Ko said.

"Thank you."

"I don't want to see you die," they said and made their way out of the dungeon.

"They're sweet," Sherrod said.

"They're saving our lives. Get ready." Aaliyah pulled herself up from the floor.

"I don't think I'm strong enough," Sherrod said.

"We just need a little fight. You distract them, I'll knock out."

Sherrod nodded and got up. She wished she had some power she could use, anything she could do instead of asking him to push himself. But she had nothing but her hands. Some champion she was.

They waited, gathering what strength they could. Aaliyah felt an unnatural breeze rustling through the dungeon.

It was the same air mage from before. She stopped short and looked confused when she saw the open cell doors. Aaliyah nodded to Sherrod and he stumbled forward, tossing a small flame at their captor. She darted to one side, using air to push the flames away from her. While she was distracted, Aaliyah shoved the mage face first into the wall.

The mage moaned as she fell. Aaliyah kicked the mage in the back of the head until she went limp. Afterward, Aaliyah gasped for breath, and fell against the wall. She locked eyes with Sherrod and nodded.

Aaliyah took one more swig of her water. She cracked her neck and motioned for Sherrod to follow her. The corridor was clear as they went.

"General," Sherrod said, pointing to an arrow on the wall,

painted in red clay at a child's height. The arrow pointed down. Ko had prepared for this.

Aaliyah had never seen this stairway before. They made their way down the steps. They seemed to go on forever. Several times Aaliyah had to stop, her limbs still weak from lack of food or water. Sherrod stayed at her back, one hand on her shoulder and the other braced against the wall.

"Aaliyah?" Helima's voice was a welcome sound in the darkness.

"Yes. We're here."

"Just a little further," Helima said.

She stood on a small dock beside a little dingy bouncing on the water. Aaliyah pulled Helima to her, hugging her tightly. Helima hugged her back, her tears wet against Aaliyah's neck.

"We're fine, we're fine," Aaliyah whispered. Helima released her and grabbed Sherrod, hugging him just as tight.

"You softie," Sherrod said.

"I hate you," Helima said, giving him a gentle shove and wiping her eyes.

They climbed into the boat and Helima started rowing. Aaliyah had no idea where they were going, but she was grateful to be free and with people she could trust.

TWELVE

Aaliyah had never been in the sewers of the city. As Helima paddled, she found herself grateful things had never been so bad for her crew. At least not bad enough to end up here. After her eyes adjusted, she saw the children in the darkness, all of them skin and bones and covered in filth. It made her stomach turn. How could Odessa not try to stop this?

Yet so many moments seemed to point to the reason. The way Odessa had been the night Aaliyah had finally killed the king. Her fervor at taking all the power Titus could offer. Her obsession with beauty at all costs.

Aaliyah should have seen this coming. She should have.

The sewer tunnel let them out into a river outside of the capital. Helima wouldn't let either of them paddle, despite the fact that it was clear fatigue was setting in. Aaliyah tried to close her eyes, but every time she did, she saw the radiance of Odessa, glowing gold behind her eyelids.

Mercy stood on the river bank, her ostentatious clothes forgone for simple black leathers. Concern marred her face until she saw them. She helped Helima haul the boat up and tie it up. Mercy looked Sherrod over briefly before she turned her attention to Aaliyah.

"Out of my sight ten minutes and you get yourself arrested for treason," she said.

Aaliyah shrugged. "You're a much better liar than me."

"Damn right I am." Mercy smiled. She wrapped an arm around Aaliyah's middle and helped her walk the rest of the way into the camp.

The river banks were covered with people from all over the city, sleeping in tents and makeshift shacks. They weren't just 'Ville residents. Some were the sort of people who would have kept out of their territory when they were kids. Still, the people stared at them, their eyes large with wonder.

Mercy led them to the center of her camp where Big Blue waited. She gestured to him and he brought two plates of food over to Aaliyah and Sherrod. Aaliyah thanked him and took a seat on one of the logs around the fire.

"How long were we in there?" Aaliyah ate greedily. Sherrod was slower but he finished his plate.

"A week, Big Blue said. "And Odessa made a serious campaign against you. She's told anyone who'll listen that you betrayed the people of Titus. Plotted to destroy what she had built. Stole from the city coffers—"

"Outright lies," Helima hissed. Aaliyah squeezed her shoulder.

"We know that," Mercy said. "Most people know that."

"But there are some that don't?" Sherrod said.

"There are some that are willing to believe her for the right price. Mostly rich merchants and mages. They see her as the real power. She's a mage and she has the right title," Mercy said.

"I followed her for less. I feel so stupid." Aaliyah couldn't look at anyone but she felt their eyes on her.

"Mistress Aaliyah," said a little voice.

Aaliyah turned her head and saw the little boy she met during her return to the city. She smiled and he sat, nestled in between her and Helima.

"Hey, little man. How're you?" Aaliyah asked.

"Tired," he said and rested his head against her arm. She rubbed his back soothingly.

"I'm sorry. Can you try to rest now?" Aaliyah said.

He had already fallen asleep, his little body turned toward

her. She sighed and rubbed his head before returning her attention to Mercy. The other woman smiled.

"You've always done your best. People see that. I told you, babe, nobody has your veracity. People lie, but you aren't responsible for being lied to if you don't know it's happening. Now that you know, you can do something different."

"Like what? What am I supposed to do?" Aaliyah said.

Mercy and Blue looked at each other. Blue ticked his head, a sign of his displeasure with whatever Mercy planned and Mercy rolled her eyes. He finally nodded, as though there had been any question he would disagree with Mercy for long.

"Our suggestion would be to get either Galavera or Oxnar to back your play." Mercy sat back with a satisfied smile.

"And what would I offer them? I have nothing to give but the promise of a loss."

"That's not true, Odessa is powerful but you're a warrior," Helima said. "The conqueror of the southern lands. The woman who slayed the iron king."

"A warrior who is powerless against her magic."

"That's what you have me for," Sherrod said, all bravado. Aaliyah shook her head.

"No offense but you're not enough. One mage against gods know how many? We can't win this fight. I'm not the leader you want. I'm useless."

"You're not useless—" Helima started.

"Against her I am. No matter what I do, she'll destroy me and everyone who sides with me."

Mercy stood up. "Are you finished?"

Blue held out his hand and Aaliyah passed him her plate. She carefully maneuvered the boy until he lay on Helima. Mercy turned away from the fire, and in the darkening evening, Aaliyah followed her to the river's edge. Mercy stopped and pointed at the silhouette of the Palace in the distance.

"What is that?"

"The palace?" Aaliyah asked.

"What is it all?"

"Titus."

"And what does Titus deserve? To continue to suffer as it has?

To have no one seek relief on their behalf?" Mercy said. "For the Champion of the realm you sure sound like an aint shit magli ready to desert her people."

"But we can't win, Mercy. My army is her army, they are sworn to her. She has mages. Mages plural. I couldn't even keep her from throwing Sherrod and I in the dungeon. I couldn't breathe."

Aaliyah stopped, her chest heaving. She couldn't breathe now. She closed her eyes.

"Aali," Mercy whispered.

"I've lost plenty of fights, Merc. I have. I don't pick fights I don't think I can win." She opened her eyes. "Odessa has beaten me in every fight we've had since we were children. She doesn't care about my feelings, she doesn't care who she has to hurt to win. She'll destroy all of Titus because I might have had the thought of taking her down. Drop it into the earth and then set it on fire. You, of all people, can't be naive enough to think Odessa won't hurt everyone to cause me pain. Hurt you. She's already destroyed everything I built. She'll burn the rest to the ground."

Aaliyah wiped a tear away. She knew what her sister was capable of. The memories swirled in her mind: her tantrums, her fingernails digging into Aaliyah's skin, the ultimatums over Mercy, and of course, throwing her into that cell.

Mercy closed the distance between them, grabbing Aaliyah's chin and moving her face so they were looking in each other's eyes. Aaliyah swallowed. Mercy relaxed her grip and let her thumb rub soothingly along Aaliyah's cheek.

"Trying is never futile, Aaliyah. You believed that when you fought for your sister. No one thought you could do this. And look what you've done! You gave her the southern lands. People laid down their swords for you. They stood with you. When you believed, so did they. That army may claim an allegiance to the crown but it was only because you did. Believe again now, and fight for yourself and for the people of Titus. You have given her an empire she cannot run. She cannot keep it without your sword. And you can take it with your hand and with your word. You're the reason people followed her and even if you lose, people deserve the right to choose which Queen they serve."

"I'm just a soldier."

"And I'm just a whore, a thief, and a murderer. The child of all three. But I still take care of my people," Mercy said. "Think of it this way: you're backing my play for Queen."

"Will you rule?" Aaliyah asked.

Mercy shook her head.

"No, probably not. But you will fight for the person I believe should rule. You will go with me to Galavera and we will get the king to back us."

"Why Galavera?"

Mercy shrugged. "I have a little more clout there."

"And what are you going to give him?" Aaliyah asked, searching Mercy's face.

The shorter woman raised an eyebrow. Aaliyah tried to look away, but Mercy slid over to maintain eye contact. She smiled. "You let me worry about what we'll offer the king. Understand?"

Aaliyah sighed. "I don't deserve you."

"But you do. You always have. You've just never believed it. There's more to you then what's Odessa's. You don't belong to her," Mercy said.

She lifted up onto her toes and Aaliyah leaned down until their lips met. Aaliyah let her hand slide around the shorter woman's waist and Mercy wrapped her arms around her neck. When Mercy lowered herself back to the ground and Aaliyah couldn't stop staring at her mouth. She tasted like honey. The general lowered her head again and Mercy chuckled, allowing her mouth to be captured by Aaliyah's tongue.

Mercy took a step back and took a deep breath. Aaliyah stepped forward, ready to chase her, but the ground beneath their feet roiled with a great cracking sound, like it was being pulled apart.. Aaliyah grabbed Mercy's arm, trying to steady them both. Screams broke out in the camp but also in the city. No one was being spared.

The great wall that protected Titus grew, taller than Aaliyah had ever seen it. She must be acting in concert with her stone mages; even Odessa wasn't powerful enough to raise the wall to such extraordinary heights. A cyclone of wind and fire whipped up behind the wall, the top of it visible from the river. Aaliyah's heart stopped as the screams grew louder, carried on the wind.

Mercy tugged her back to the camp.

"She definitely knows you're out," Helima said, climbing up onto her horse. Sherrod's face was hard as he mounted a borrowed mare.

Blue held two saddled horses, one a chestnut bay and the other a black stallion. Both animals were skittish as Mercy and Aaliyah approached. Mercy threw herself on the back of the bay. Blue handed the reins of the black stallion to Aaliyah and she pulled herself up onto its back. She ran a hand lovingly down its neck to soothe it.

"Blue, camp's in your care," Mercy said.

"I got it," Blue said, with a slight bow.

Aaliyah saw the little boy wrapped in a woman's arms. He was crying but the woman was trying to calm him. She wasn't sure she could do this, but she'd do anything for these kids to not have to live in fear. She looked at Blue and nodded. He reluctantly nodded back, she could see his feelings warring within him. He wasn't sure she could do this either.

"Return with some backup, my Queen," Blue said.

The sound of the title made Aaliyah's stomach go cold and her skin clammy. She nodded. Mercy spurred her horse and Aaliyah was grateful to get away from the beginnings of her responsibility.

THIRTEEN

The road to Galavera was not long but it was still perilous. Mercy would not allow them to put themselves in danger. They needed to avoid anyone with potential connections to the Queen: merchants, mages and soldiers alike. Avoiding all those people meant spending much of their time riding near the road but not on it. They were forced to stop at odd times, to wait out people and avoid getting too near other camps.

All the clandestine travel reminded Aaliyah of the story of how the southern lands came to be. The story went that when the world had been new there had only been three countries. The pale people of Oxnar, the golden people of Galavera and the deep brown people of Titus. They'd lived in harmony for years, moving easily between the nations blissfully. No one agreed on which nation started it but word began to spread that Oxnar wanted nothing to do with the other two nations and they were willing to go to war. Galavera and Titus, selfish little countries, began to prepare for war from both of the other countries. Why they didn't band together had never been clear. A group of Titans, Oxnarans, and Galaverans decided they wanted nothing to do with the wars and strife of these large nations, and so in the night they moved large portions of the courts in secret to the south, forming the many small tribes of the southern lands seeking a place where they could live peacefully.

The war itself came to naught, but the physical separation that it fostered lived on. Despite that, their cultures were deeply influenced by the years of peaceful mixing. Galavera was still the jewel of their continent, magic flourishing within its borders and as common as air. The King was said to be hard but fair, powerful and kind. Aaliyah knew that if she'd brought the army of Titus there they would have battled valiantly but the King of Galavera would have crushed them mightily.

Why would he bother to aid her now when she had truly nothing to offer except her arm? A useless arm at that.

Throughout the journey, Aaliyah couldn't fight the overwhelming feeling that this effort wasn't worth it. The King would send them on their way, or worse take them prisoner, to offer Odessa and gain her good favor. And the thought of what Odessa would do with them once she had them... Helima and Sherrod didn't need that. They could have been living excellent lives at home, if they simply let Aaliyah sit in the dungeon. Odessa would have eventually let Sherrod go. Aaliyah kept her dark thoughts to herself.

She noticed that Sherrod was unusually quiet too. Aaliyah imagined he might be thinking the same things she was. She knew there were at least twenty girls back home he could be with. He could have been the General of Titus's army. She noticed him avoiding her, staying at the edge of their camps and riding at the back of the line. For all his bravado, she would not have been surprised if he'd run back and begged for forgiveness.

Helima was quiet too, but it didn't bother Aaliyah because that was just her way. Even when they'd lived on the streets, Helima never voiced her disapproval or her happiness. She'd learned to keep herself carefully neutral. At strange moments, Aaliyah would catch her staring, studying. She had no idea what Helima could be thinking.

Mercy avoided her. She said she wasn't, but every time Aaliyah tried to get her alone Mercy managed to find another task to accomplish. Aaliyah felt isolated and confused. For all the betrayal, she missed Odessa's loving caresses and the long letters

Odessa had written while Aaliyah battled for her. Here she was all alone.

"Eat," Helima said when they stopped on the second day. Aaliyah accepted the portion of rations that Helima handed her and tried to focus on the texture of it in her mouth. "You look like a child."

"*You* look like a child," Aaliyah said and Helima rolled her eyes.

"She's not wrong, you did used to make that face a lot," Mercy said with a mischievous smile.

"I meant to ask," Sherrod said, picking at his own meal. "How do you all know each other?"

Helima looked at Aaliyah. They really hadn't told him much about their childhood. Hadn't felt it necessary. But if he was going to fight and possibly die with her, he deserved to know.

"You know the Queen and I were street kids," Aaliyah said. Sherrod nodded. "My mother took Odessa on when her mother died in a brothel in the southern lands. But that didn't last long. She left us at an orphanage when I was three. Couldn't stand Odessa's tantrums. She was powerful even then. Orphanage couldn't give us much. So I started stealing."

"She was bad at it. Obvious. My father thought it was funny," Mercy said.

"Your father?"

"Prince of thieves. My old man ran the 'Ville back in the day." Mercy knelt beside the fire and stoked it with more wood.

Sherrod's eyes widened. He looked up at Aaliyah and then back down at the flame, coaxing it with his power.

"Her father trained me in the blade. I held corners for him for a long time," Aaliyah said.

"Corners?" Sherrod said. Helima snorted.

"Spoiled ass. Adu spots. Whore houses. Whatever the Prince wanted, Aaliyah kept," Helima said simply. "Then I wandered in to help."

"Something like that," Mercy said and she stood in the glow of the fire. "It's funny, you always had a knack for leadership. My father used to say that. The corner boys would follow you anywhere you sent them. Blue hated that."

Aaliyah shrugged but she could feel their eyes on her. This was different. Helima threw a stick at her and she looked up.

"I'll follow," she said simply.

Aaliyah nodded, trying not to cry as she thought of the undersized girl with the too big head on her shoulders that the other corner boys had pushed around. Aaliyah had given her some food but expected her to run off.

"I got shit to do, magli. Get gone," Aaliyah had said, something like that, trying to sound as cool as the others.

Helima had straightened her spine and raised her chin. "I'll follow."

And she had. All these years, she'd followed Aaliyah into one kind of trouble or another. She turned her head and wiped a stray tear from her eye.

When she was a little more composed, Aaliyah looked at Sherrod and found him watching her. "One more thing you should know before you follow me any further," Aaliyah said.

"What?" Sherrod took a sip of water.

"My girl in the palace?" Aaliyah said. "She's my sister."

The choking gasp that Sherrod made was actually a little funny for a moment. Aaliyah waited, straightening her back. She could be judged a fool for many things but she wouldn't be judged about this.

They'd been judged before. The Prince of Thieves, when he'd found out, had been ready to throw them back to the street but for Mercy's intervention. They may not be together now but that relationship was...sacred.

"Guess there's no way we were sharing then," he said between strangled breaths.

It was the first time Aaliyah had laughed in a long time.

FOURTEEN

They arrived in Galavera after three long nights. Aaliyah had been there only once before, and then in the dark of night, in order to get a better look at the forces of the king. Now though, in the full light of day with people milling about it, seemed a different place. The people of Galavera were brown, but in different shades then the people of Titus. They were olive brown with wavy dark hair and a multitude of eye colors. As they rode through the capital, people stopped to look at them. Mercy seemed unaware of the eyes on them, she rode with her head held high and facing forward. Aaliyah couldn't help but notice people staring at her.

"Lady!"

Aaliyah stopped her horse.

The woman who cried out was young, brown skinned, and wearing her hair in long braids. "Forgive me, lady, have you come from Titus?"

"Yes, sis," Aaliyah said. The woman smiled up at her, coming to rest one hand on the horse.

"Aaliyah, don't stop," Mercy said, turning back enough to look at them.

"Is it true what they're saying?"

"Who's 'they'?" Aaliyah asked.

"The merchants escaping from Titus. Refugees," the woman said.

"What are they saying?"

"That the capital is in flames, the city was being burned by the criminal General Aaliyah. That she's on her way here to—"

"Be silent, girl." Mercy forced her horse between Aaliyah and the woman. "You don't know what you're talking about."

The woman stumbled away from them, eying them suspiciously. Aaliyah swallowed down the bile that rose in her throat. The capital in flames? How many people had Odessa killed in Aaliyah's name?

Mercy led her through the city but Aaliyah had no idea where they were going. They stopped when they reached a large boarding house, in the shadow of the palace. She jumped down from her horse's back and led them into the stable. A groom jumped up when she came in.

"Madame Mercy," the groom greeted her.

"Take care of the horses, Walead," she said in a clipped tone. "Is your master at home?"

"He is in the garden Madame. Not to be disturbed by any member of the house," The groom answered, holding Aaliyah's horse while she climbed down. He looked at her and stopped. "You're...General Aaliyah."

"I am," Aaliyah said. He stared a moment longer and then looked at Mercy.

"I suppose you're not a member of the household," he said carefully, and Mercy nodded.

Helima and Sherrod gave their mounts to the man and they followed Mercyinto the large house. A housekeeper rushed into the main hall to meet them. Mercy strode past even as the housekeeper tried to stop her.

"Madame Mercedes, my master is happy always to have you in his house, perhaps you could be kind enough to wait in the parlor and not disturb him in the garden." The housekeeper 's voice got louder as Mercy continued through the house into an elaborate garden with large overgrown trees, flowering vines and a water fountain.

The air here was filed with the sound of hushed grunts and

laughter, melding with the sound of birds crying out. Aaliyah noticed an ornate covered sitting area. There were four posts and the posts had layers of sheer curtains. Beyond them Aaliyah could see the outline of two figures, wrapped in an embrace. She reached out for Mercy, trying to slow her progress, but Mercy just pressed forward.

"Master!" the housekeeper shouted.

Mercy stopped just short of the curtained area and waited. Aaliyah followed close behind while Sherrod and Helima hung back, standing ready closer to the house.

They heard a curse behind the curtains, and then a laugh. The figures stood, , their figure becoming more clear as they grew closer. One of them moved the curtain aside enough to stick their head through.

"What is causing such a disturbance..." the man trailed off, his eyes focusing on Aaliyah. His face went slack with shock, his eyes growing large.

Aaliyah stared back. She had never met him but she recognized him immediately. He could only be her father, Akil. He had her eyes and nose, though his lips were fuller than hers and his skin darker still. His hair was long and loc'd, peppered with gray throughout. He'd haphazardly pulled a robe across his shoulders and now he put it fully on, covering his nudity.

"What is it, habibi?" Another masculine voice called from beyond the curtain.

"My daughter, omri," Akil said. There was movement beyond the curtain and the man pushed it open more. He was equally handsome, his olive brown skin slick with sweat. His black hair was cut short and a long scar crossed his face. His hazel eyes studied both Aaliyah and Mercy.

Mercy dropped to one knee but Aaliyah found she couldn't make her body work. Her father was standing in front of her. Her father.

He waved to the housekeeper, causing her to run from where she had stopped on the path.

She knelt before him, shooting Mercy a hostile look that she didn't see. "Master?"

"Please make my guests comfortable in the parlor. Bring them tea and food. The King and I will join you shortly."

"As you will it," the housekeeper said.

Mercy stood and Akil gave her a look before he returned his attention to Aaliyah. He gave her a small smile and she tried to return it. Aaliyah found the will to move, following the housekeeper back into the house. She caught Helima's eye and the other woman raised an eyebrow. So here was the other half of her identity: Akil, her father, lover of the King of Galavera.

FIFTEEN

The housekeeper, Rhia, was more than happy to bring them both hot tea and iced tea, ice water and even wine for Mercy, though she mumbled something under her breath when she handed it to her. She was warm to everyone else, bringing them plates of a sweet, flaky dessert and a more savory dish that tasted of spices and meat. Things Aaliyah had never seen before outnumbered those she had. Sherrod and Helima ate with relish but the food on Aaliyah's tongue tasted of ash. Mercy watched her from behind her wine glass but said nothing.

When Akil and the King, Omar, made their way into the room, Aaliyah couldn't help but stare. They were so much alike in their features that she felt like she was watching herself, though his movements were more graceful than her own. Akil sat beside the King and poured him first iced tea and then wine. He made the King a small plate of food, poured himself some tea and sat back on the sofa. He looked at Aaliyah and then at Mercy.

"What happened, Mercedes? Something must have, for you to prompt this reunion." Akil sipped his tea.

"Odessa has named Aaliyah a traitor."

The King's gaze was appraising as he took her measure. "And are you a traitor?"

"If asking why my sister abandoned her promises makes me a traitor, then yes," Aaliyah said.

"That doesn't seem treasonous to me," Akil said quietly. The King put a hand on the back of his neck.

"You met that girl, habibi. Paranoid and power hungry. But she told me you were one of her greatest assets. The Champion of Titus. Conqueror of the Southern lands." The King returned his attention to Aaliyah. "So she called you a traitor and you came running to Galavera. Did you seek to find your father's favor? To move my hand by your blood bond? Are you just as power hungry as your sister?"

"I didn't even know he was here." Aaliyah met Akil's eye and he squirmed in his seat. He looked down into his tea cup.

Mercy cleared her throat. "I brought her here without telling her what we would find. I thought you might back her in a play to be Queen, your Majesty,."

The King laughed. "Odessa is quite powerful. A stone mage of great strength. When she came to me, I told her nothing she offered me worth an alliance, but now that I see you, you are quite tempting. Still, I have no intention of going against her."

"*I'm* tempting?" Aaliyah asked. "Mercy said she offered herself in marriage."

"No," the King said, leaning forward. "She offered me *you*. At the time I didn't know you looked so much like your father."

Mercy looked down into her wine glass.

"Omri, please," Akil said. The King stroked his thumb along her father's neck. He pulled Akil closer against his body and kissed the top of his head.

"I'm only teasing, habibi. No one could replace you. But you must admit, it's like looking at yourself in the glass."

"Odessa knew you lived here?" Aaliyah asked.

Akil looked a little embarrassed. "I met her on one of her visits. The King walked her as far as my gate. She must have seen your face in mine. She told me whose daughter she was, asked if I knew about you and...told me I hadn't missed much. We didn't speak again. Omar has told me everything about what she's said in her meetings with him."

"I met him after that, when I was trying to find out what

Odessa was up to," Mercy said. "I told him more about you."

Aaliyah noticed how still Sherrod and Helima had gone. How intently they were listening. She tried to meet Helima's eye but she was studying her tea.

Aaliyah looked at Akil. He nodded his head slowly.

"Your mother never told me about you. And I..." he paused, seeming to consider his next words carefully. He cleared his throat. "Even if she had I don't know that I would have been a part of your life. I was young and selfish and...I didn't love your mother. We—"

Omar rested a hand on his.

Akil smiled up at the King. "Coming here, loving Omar. It changed my priorities. What I cared about. Mercy and my meeting when we did was advantageous. I...I realised I had likely missed my opportunity to have children," Akil said. "I'm too old now to start from scratch. But I wanted someone to love and she brought me you. The great warrior who was conquering the southern lands and ended the tyrannical reign of the old King. I was proud of you."

Aaliyah stood up, Helima and Akil rising as well. "I need some air."

Aaliyah waved off Helima. She could hear Akil following close behind her as she strode out of the room. When she reached the garden, instead of turning toward the sitting area she followed the maze of the path, aware of him at her back. Eventually she reached a fountain laden with sweet smelling flowers and sat on the stone bench beside it. She waited for Akil to sit beside her but he didn't, instead perching on the edge of the fountain, one hand toying with the flowers. He plucked a bloom and sniffed it, pretending not to notice her.

They sat in silence. Aaliyah took deep, long, shuddering breaths. She was calm. She was calm. She was calm. It didn't stop the tears from running down her face. She couldn't stop the sob that ricocheted through her chest. Akil sat at her feet. He didn't touch her, his hands gripping the flower too tight.

"I'm so sorry, Aaliyah."

"For what?" she asked, wiping her face. Her father had never known about her. She'd lived on the street, been forced to steal to eat, and he had never *known*.

"For all that's happened. Everyone around you has betrayed you in one way or another and you are the only one who's blameless."

"I'm not blameless."

Akil looked up at her. "What did you do?"

"I backed her every move. I fought every battle she put before me, without question. I knew her better than anyone and I still made her a Queen. Mercy thinks power is Odessa's drug. She's not wrong. I knew that. And I gave her more and more and more. She even has the southern lands now. Maybe if I hadn't been such a fool, Mother could have..." She closed her eyes, pulling away from the pain of that thought. "It doesn't matter. I must love women who lie. Even when I know they're liars. Look at Mercy. She never told me about you."

"You were gone."

She opened her eyes, wiping away more tears. "It changes nothing."

"You acted from a place of love. Who of the rest of us can say otherwise," Akil said.

"You love the King, don't you?" Aaliyah asked.

He looked down at the flower. "Yes, but I still acted from a selfish place. I could have stayed with your mother instead of chasing my heart across the kingdoms. For my part of it, I'm sorry. That will never be enough but I hope it's something."

Aaliyah nodded and he smiled up at her, lowering his hand to her lap and twining their fingers together. They lapsed into silence again. The water in the fountain and the breeze through the leaves were the only sounds. Aaliyah pressed the heel of her palms to her eyes, trying to block out everything. She'd defeated warlords and killed a King but *this* was all too much.

"What did you come here for?" Akil asked.

"Mercy thinks that I will make a good Queen for the people of Titus. She thought King Omar could be persuaded to provide me troops."

"I know what Mercy wants. She's shared enough. Do you want to be Queen?" Akil asked. "You could just as easily live here with me, safe and sound. Omar would find a use for you in his army I'm sure. You could become a soldier here. Perhaps work your way up to General again."

"I don't want to be Queen, but I can't leave the people of Titus and the southern lands to suffer. Not when I promised them things would be different," Aaliyah said. "Even if I'm not their Queen, things have to be different."

Akil smiled and stood up. He pulled her to her feet and kissed her fingers. The skin felt strange as she let him lead them more slowly back down the path.

"Mercy's right. You'll be a great Queen. If only because you'll do it to serve your people and not yourself. Your Odessa craves power and her enemies on their knees. It's an impossible task that never ends." Akil said. "As for troops, you'll have them."

"You'll convince the King?"

Akil laughed. "He won't require any convincing. He told me if you were here to go against Odessa he would gladly support you. Apparently, he didn't like her attitude, nor her disparaging remarks about me. He just likes to antagonize Mercedes."

He led them back into the house where Mercy and King Omar were in the middle of heated disagreement. Helima's eyes sparkled with humor but she sobered quickly, when Aaliyaand Akil came in the room. Sherrod too sat up, taking in their joined hands. King Omar held out his hand and Akil went, releasing her with a small squeeze, settling himself beside the king once more.

"All settled?" the King asked, his hand coming to rest possessively against Akil's neck.

"Mmm, once you promise her the use of your army for her campaign then yes, we will be," Akil said.

King Omar smirked."Is that all it will take? Does the girl even want to be Queen?"

"I don't," Aaliyah said.

"You see? Why should I give such a useless person access to my warriors?"

"Omri—"

"I'm not..." Aaliyah stopped herself, clearing her throat before she spoke. "I have no power, your majesty, only my sword. And my word. I don't want to be queen, but as everyone keeps telling me, I owe it to the people to fight for them."

King Omar tilted his head, eying her.

"She can do this, Omar, she can defeat her," Mercy said. "All it takes is—"

"Enough," King Omar said. "You know, Aaliyah, they say no one's steel is as powerful as yours. If you can defeat me in a fight then I will give you a hundred soldiers."

"Omar—" Mercy and Akil said in unison.

"Fifty soldiers and fifty mages," Aaliyah said. Omar smiled.

"Every soldier in Galavera is a mage, General. One hundred soldiers, each wielding the great powers. But you have to beat me first."

He held out his hand, and Aaliyah took a deep breath before she took it. "Deal."

Akil led them out to an area of the garden that had been paved smooth. King Omar took one side of the paved circle and Aaliyah took another. He removed his shirt, revealing a muscular torso crossed with pale scars. Aaliyah pulled off her over shirt, leaving only a sweat soaked undershirt and her binding.

Mercy stood beside her as she stretched. She looked nervous, though she said nothing. Sherrod vibrated with energy, bouncing on his toes.

"Are you sure you should do this?" he asked. "We've been on the road for days and you spent days in a cell before that."

"I don't have a choice. We need his backing," Aaliyah said.

Sherrod opened his mouth to say something else but Helima shot him a look. She drew her blade and handed it over to Aaliyah. She grabbed Aaliyah's hand and held her eye.

"We'll support you either way. Galavera or no," she said.

She turned back to the King. Omar gave Akil a quick kiss on the cheek and stepped forward to meet Aaliyah in the circle.

"Shall we go till first blood?" Omar offered.

"No," Aaliyah said. "Till the death blow."

"Aaliyah!" Mercy hissed, grabbing Aaliyah's bicep and trying to pull her away. Her teeth were gritted and her eyes wild. "What do you think you're doing?"

Omar laughed. "I like your style, General. Of course, no one will die today. And whatever injuries can be healed."

The two of them squared off. A calm settled over Aaliyah. She knew how to do this, how to fight. How to win. They circled each other, sizing each other up. Aaliyah danced forward, not really seeking to land a blow but trying to get an estimate of the man she faced. The King shook off her blow, side stepping the strike.

"Is this how you are in battle? Nervous and shy?"

Aaliyah didn't let herself be baited. She watched the man as he moved, noting his strength and his obvious skill. He struck. To anyone else it would have looked wild but Aaliyah saw through that; he wanted to see how strong she was. She spun beneath the strike, using his own motion to knock him away and put her own blow under his arm.

Omar ducked back, reaching beneath his arm to pull away a bloody hand. He smiled. "I bet you're wishing you'd chosen first blood."

"No, sir. You want to see what I'm made of, I'll show you."

Omar struck again, no longer wanting to play games. Aaliyah deflected. His attacks came fast and furious. He wanted her tired. She had no time to play his game. To win, she needed to change the rules.

She knocked his blade away and then kicked the open canvas of his stomach, doubling him over. She brought her blade down toward the back of his neck but the ground rumbled and she was knocked flat on her back. She rolled away from where she'd landed, narrowly avoiding Omar's strike. She jumped up, slashing at him again and nicking his arm. This time wind knocked her back, and she flipped away from him again.

"I forgot," Omar said. "Magli, aren't you? Not a lick of power. What are you going to do against her? Stone filled, isn't she?"

The ground rumbled again and Aaliyah stumbled back. She tried to find her center but the paving stones reached out to trip her. Her sword went flying and she landed with a thud. Omar's blade moved relentlessly toward her neck. Her resolve slipped. Odessa would do the same soon. It didn't matter if she had a hundred men or a thousand. And then she caught sight of Helima. Hel, who had backed her since that night, all those years ago. Who didn't seem to care whether they lived or died together so long as they were still a family.

Aaliyah rolled.

She flipped onto her front and jumped up on raised stone, striking Omar in the nose. He grunted and stumbled back. Aaliyah put her knee into his chest, and then again into his groin. She could hear shouting in her ears but no one moved. She kicked Omar's hand and he released his blade, landing flat and hard on his back. She reached out to grab his blade and felt another against her throat. She stilled.

"You're beaten," Omar said in a hoarse voice.

"I lost, but I'm not beaten," Aaliyah said.

She backed away until she felt a firm hand at her shoulder. Helima turned her, looking Aaliyah over for any scratches.

"You were alright," Helima said. "Bit slow."

"You'd have done better," Aaliyah said.

"Probably."

Aaliyah turned back to Omar where Akil was clucking over his wounds. The King stared her down before breaking free of Akil's hold. "You were even better than I thought."

"Thank you. We'll get out of your hair now," Aaliyah said, nodding to Mercy, Sherrod and Helima.

"There's no need for you to leave," Omar said. "I won't give you a hundred soldiers. You lost and I don't reward losing."

"Of course."

"Enough games, Omri." Akil crossed his arms.

"I'll give you five. Two archers, and three guards— "

"And I will go too," Akil said.

Omar looked down at him, his eyes bulging. "You have not been in battle in years. In armor even. What exactly will you do?"

"Support my daughter in her bid to be Queen. However I can."

Omar gritted his teeth. "You would do better supporting her from here."

"Omri." Akil raised an eyebrow and Aaliyah bit her lip. She'd so rarely stood her ground with Odessa but this must have been what her face looked like when she did.

Omar sighed.

"Habibi." He turned to Aaliyah. "Two Archers, three guards, an old man and a King. Will that be alright with you?"

"Yes...I...thank you for your faith," Aaliyah said. She took a deep breath, letting it out slowly and closed her eyes. Relief washed over her even as her stomach twisted. Here was yet another person to disappoint.

"You've earned it."

King Omar held out his hand and Aaliyah took it. They shook hands and Aaliyah lowered her head. Omar released her and pulled Akil toward the house. Aaliyah sighed. Five people was nothing compared to the hundreds Odessa had on her side.

"Four Galavarans is good, we can do a lot with that," Sherrod said optimistically.

"We'll make it work," Helima said.

And for all her bluster and need to come to Galavera, Mercy was silent. It didn't make Aaliyah any more optimistic about their chances.

SIXTEEN

Akil offered them beds for as long as they wished to stay and rest but Aaliyah could only agree to one night. Aaliyah felt strange preparing to sleep in her father's house. What would it have been like to grow up here, with everything she ever wanted within her grasp at all times? Would her father have been attentive to her or would she have constantly been competing with the King? She hoped not—it didn't seem like a battle she could have won.

There was a knock on her door that pulled her away from her thoughts.When she opened it, Mercy stood in the doorway, fresh from a bath, her twists pulled high on top of her head and only a thin robe to cover her. She smiled coyly but Aaliyah recognized it for what it was, the sort of look she wore with a client, never reaching her eyes.

"Wassup?"

"May I come in?" Mercy asked.

Aaliyah stepped aside and Mercy entered. She looked around at the bedroom and Aaliyah somehow felt self-conscious about it even though it wasn't hers. Mercy settled into a chair by the fire, kicking off her little slippers and stretching her toes in front of the warmth.

"Are you angry with me?" Mercy asked.

Aaliyah sat down in the chair opposite her. Mercy's eyes focused on the flame engulfed wood instead of her face. Aaliyah sighed.

"What do you think?"

"I would be, if I were you."

"Well, I am."

"I should have told you about him, and about what she'd done. I should have—"

"Why didn't you?"

Mercy shrugged. "I don't know. Maybe you were safer this way. You didn't know enough to be hurt."

"Maybe you were."

"What?"

Aaliyah stood up and crossed the room until she stood in front of Mercy. "Maybe you were afraid if you told me all this, I wouldn't believe you. That you'd drive me into Odessa's arms and lose me forever."

Mercy chuckled derisively. "Who says I want you?"

"Odessa. And she may be wrong about a lot but I don't think her jealousy is misplaced. She's always been the smarter of the two of us."

"You're not dumb," Mercy said.

"You're avoiding the point."

Mercy bit her lip. Looked up at Aaliyah and then down at her hands. "And if she's not wrong? If I...If I do want you?"

Aaliyah knelt down in front of Mercy's chair. "I wish you'd say that."

Mercy took a long deep breath in and then a long slow breath out. She repeated it twice more. Her voice cracked. "I want you."

Aaliyah didn't hesitate, she surged forward, pressing her mouth to Mercy's, seeking purchase there and finding it. Aaliyah licked into Mercy's mouth and Mercy moaned in answer, allowing Aaliyah to overtake her.

Aaliyah stood, lifting Mercy up, and leading them mostly blindly to the bed. She spared half a thought for the open door but then Mercy moaned again and she didn't care. She heaved Mercy onto the bed. When Mercy's robe fell open, Aaliyah pulled away to look at the smooth brown skin that had been exposed, running her fingers down Mercy's sternum. The bone mage shivered. Aaliyah pushed the robe the rest of the way down Mercy's shoulders, baring all her skin to the cool air and making little bumps crop up on her skin.

Aaliyah worshiped every inch of her.

SEVENTEEN

The ride back to Titus took four days, Akil's lack of travel over the years slowing their progress. The two guards and the archer were all skilled soldiers and they seemed to take the slow progress in stride. For Aaliyah, it only built up her anxiety.

Seventeen days since Aaliyah's return from the southern lands and she couldn't feel any more different than the last time she'd been standing at the bend in the road, waiting for the city to come into view. She wore old armor, a remnant from Akil's days in the military. The leather was studded with onyx, which made it stronger but also heavier than Aaliyah's usual armor. In the distance, the high walls still stood strong, and plumes of black smoke drifted into the sky. She couldn't see what was burning but she could smell the acrid scent.

Akil leaned against a tree nearby. His own armor was heavier then he was used to, though Aaliyah thought Galavera's jade wrapped leather was hardly a great burden. Jade wasn't particularly strong but it warded off magic use. The King had no shortage of worried glances but her father would have none of his fussing; he had been a warrior too in his day and he wanted to be respected as such. It was strange but she liked the two of them together. For all she would have preferred to have a father that raised her, she could see that the love between Omar and Akil would not be thwarted by anyone.

"General," King Omar said as he climbed down from his horse to stand beside her. "Do you wish to send a scout?"

Aaliyah looked at Helima, the other woman's eyes focused in the direction of the capital. "Helima."

Helima turned her attention to Aaliyah, but it was only with her eyes. Aaliyah could see what she was thinking of, as though Jalil stood right in front of them. "General?"

"Change clothes and get into the city. Find out what you can," Aaliyah said.

"Shouldn't I go, General?" Sherrod asked, and by all accounts he was right. He was the lowest ranking officer present in her service.

"Helima's going," Aaliyah said.

"Wait," Mercy said. "Look."

They turned back to the road and someone was coming around the bend at a run. As they watched, one boulder then two flew through the sky from beyond the wall in an attempt to hit the runner. Aaliyah looked at Sherrod and he nodded, taking his horse at a gallop to reach them. Sherrod closed the distance and pulled the runner up onto the back of his horse in one smooth fluid movement.

"Is that a uniform?" King Omar said.

"A soldier," Mercy said.

"Seems likely," Aaliyah said. "Helima, change anyway. Just in case whoever this is isn't helpful."

Helima disappeared into the roadside brush without another word. Sherrod slowed his horse and helped the young woman down. Aaliyah recognized the private. It felt like months since Aaliyah had seen her that morning in the bunk and she had looked young and bright eyed. The girl's green eyes had lost some of their luster and her red hair was dull. Her skin was covered in bruises and cuts. She grabbed Aaliyah's arm and tried to smile. She collapsed to her knees and tried to catch her breath. Aaliyah helped Sherrod move her beneath Akil's shady tree. Mercy brought water and the private began to drink.

"I knew you'd be back, General. You wouldn't leave us to the stone bitch." She flinched as Akil adjusted her right arm; it was at least dislocated.

"Never that. Tell me your name, Private?"

"Omolara, General."

"You've served me well. You deserve a promotion." Aaliyah smiled. The tears the young woman had been fighting fell down her cheeks and Aaliyah pulled her into her chest. She sobbed for a few minutes before she pulled back.

"I don't deserve anything, General. We couldn't stop her from hurting people," Omolara said.

"Tell me what's been going on."

"You felt the quake?" she asked.

"We did."

"She sealed the city. She's raised a hundred men high wall around the perimeter. She keeps mages on the towers to maintain it and to attack anyone who tries to go over." She closed her eyes for a moment before beginning again. "Most of the people were starving already, it's getting worse. There have been a lot of casualties, General. People trying to escape. Everyone's afraid of her."

"Who's still loyal to her?" Sherrod said.

"Mostly the upper level mages. The strongest ones think if the Queen squashes you then they'll have a place of honor in her kingdom. When she heard you'd fled to Galavera, she figured you'd be back with support. And if she defeats even the smallest contingent from Galavera..."

Helima cursed. "She'll spin as having defeated one of the great remaining powers."

"How did you get out, Omolara?" Mercy asked.

"A few of the rebel mages are anxious. They knew you'd be back soon. They thought it was better to have a soldier as an ally," Omolara said. "Most of the soldiers have been taken into custody by the mages. Locked up in the Palace."

"And the Queen?" Aaliyah asked. Mercy put her hand on her shoulder.

"She's just sitting on the throne all the time, giving orders and destroying things. They say she's torn down near every wall of the palace. Doesn't care who gets hurt by the rubble either. But she never leaves that throne. She's waiting, I think."

"Waiting for what?" Akil asked.

"For the General. They have strict orders on the wall, you're to go to her." Omolara took a deep breath. "She gets to kill you."

Aaliyah moved away from the group. She shouldn't be surprised. She shouldn't at all. Perhaps if she were in Odessa's shoes, she might want her dead too. But it wasn't true. No matter what, she couldn't want Odessa dead. Mercy wrapped her arms around her and she let herself be held a moment before putting her war face on. She turned back to where Omolara lay, being bandaged by Akil and Sherrod.

"Mercy, send a man to get Blue and any men from the 'Ville who are willing to fight." Aaliyah said. She turned to the King where he'd tucked himself beside Akil. "Your highness, I need your archer."

EIGHTEEN

The message she sent over was simple: Lower the wall and allow them in, no harm would come to those who did not stand against her. She didn't honestly expect for Odessa to comply. But it was a courtesy she gave every place she was about to conquer. One last opportunity to set their swords aside and avoid a battle.

Some of the corner boys joined them on the road, but Blue wasn't among them. If Mercy was bothered she hid it well. She rode beside Aaliyah, flexing her fingers. Aaliyah could feel the sizzle of magic around her.

Omar was clearly anxious about the message. He looked from Aaliyah to where the wall would be when they rounded the bend and back again so many times he was going to get a neck ache. Aaliyah didn't care. They were doing it her way. She allowed them until the sun was high in the sky overhead and then she rallied the troops. She didn't want to kill anyone if she didn't have to.

They took the curve in the road and Aaliyah saw Titus again with new eyes. The wall now obscured everything but the very tops of the spires of the palace and the tiny figures of the mages on the wall. Aaliyah called a halt when they were near enough to the wall that she could be heard. The archer, who was also an air mage, stepped forward to amplify her voice.

"People of Titus, my name is General Aaliyah. You know me. I am a daughter of your streets. I have no desire to harm the people of my city," she called out. The mages on the wall began to move toward the center, drawn by her voice. "I have returned here to the home of my heart to bring you peace. The peace I promised five years ago. Food for all people. Homes for all people. A leader who cares for each of you, whose concern is your well-being. You would honor me by choosing me. But if you will not choose me, I will still fight for you. Allow me to end this pain. Allow me to remove the tyrant from your midst. Lay down your arms, lower the wall and I will protect you from one who will not."

There had been no wall the day she had killed the king but she had given a similar speech in Odessa's name. There had been people who had sat down, who had cheered her coming. There had been people who had fought, most of them had died. She waited now, her horse anxious, his ears flicking back and forth. She missed Hassim.

The ground rumbled and shifted, lurching the group forward. It shifted again and sent them backward. Aaliyah sighed and whistled.

Arrows soared through the sky hitting mage after mage assembled on the wall. They took off running but Galavera's archers were marksmen. Mages fell and fell so until the wall exploded in a spray of rock dust. Aaliyah whistled again and the army moved forward.

The streets were silent as they marched through. The only people on the street had no homes and they kept their heads bowed and their eyes down. A few mages from the wall sat beside the large hole, their faces pressed to the ground in obeisance. As Aaliyah crossed the threshold of the city, the murmurs began.

"Bless you."

"Gods bless."

"May the gods protect you."

Tears shone in Aaliyah's eyes as she moved through the city unchallenged. She could see the faces in windows, their lips moving furiously in what seemed to be silent prayer. The city was choosing her.

"Stop there, General!"

Aaliyah returned her gaze to the road ahead. Rakheem stood in her path. He was flanked by a water mage, in deep blue robes and a bone mage, in stark white. Rakheem smiled as rocks swirled over his head, ready to hurtle at them at any moment.

"We don't need to do this. There will be a place for you here, all of you." Aaliyah said. Beside her, Mercy tensed. Sherrod drew fire into his hand.

"We don't want to live in your kingdom. We like this one just fine," he shouted. Aaliyah nodded and readied her spear.

"Mercy, Sherrod," Aaliyah said.

The stone mage charged her, rock and dust swirling, he tore a piece of house free from it's fitting and threw it at her. She knocked it aside, conscious of those around her. Sherrod took off after the water mage, throwing balls of flame at their heels. Merc's fingers danced as she tore the bone mages limbs open. The mage screamed in agony with each elegant flick . Helima moved quickly, getting people out of the way. Aaliyah let the stone mage attack, let him throw rock after rock, let them grow in size. She simply deflected and defended, waiting patiently for the hubris she knew would come.

When he attempted to heave up the whole house front, to throw the entire solid wall at her, she found her in. Aaliyah thrust forward and dropped to one knee, using the weight of the armor to propel her. She disemboweled him with her spear, watching as his entrails formed a pile at his feet. The house front fell, shattering into many pieces of rubble.

"Helima?" Aaliyah caught her breath.

"No deaths besides the mages. A few injuries," she answered.

"I'll see to them," Sherrod said, wiping his hands on his pants. The water mage laid still along the edge of the road. Aaliyah nodded. Mercy sauntered over. Aaliyah could no longer see the palace bone mage and she said a silent prayer for his soul.

"This is the strangest invasion I have ever seen," Omar said. "I could have stayed home."

"Well, you've never seen the Champion of Titus invade,"

Helima said. "Remind me to tell you about when we took Aquis."

Aaliyah smiled as she returned her attention to the Palace ahead of her. Omar was right, though. They walked through the remainder of the city unchallenged, amidst hundreds of blessings murmured by the people. When they reached the inner wall of the Palace, Aaliyah stopped, horrified at what she saw.

Hanging from the wall was Blue's body, his arms tied behind his back, his legs tied together. Aaliyah cut the rope that held him to the wall and Helima caught him. Mercy tore Blue's body from Helima's arms, sobbing.

Aaliyah and Helima looked at each other. Aaliyah knew exactly what she was thinking."Find him Hel," Aaliyah whispered. Helima took off into the palace.

Aaliyah redirected her attention, wrapping an arm around Mercy's shoulders."She killed him," Mercy said, tears streaming down her face, cradling Blue's still body. "She killed him."

Aaliyah looked up at the gate. There were others she recognized, people she could have guessed would support her. Including the mage who had freed her from the Dungeon

She couldn't look at Blue's face. He may have hated her but she wouldn't have wanted this for him. "You don't have to go in with me," Aaliyah said.

"I want to see her when she dies. I want to burn the body," Mercy whispered.

Aaliyah nodded. Akil came forward and took Blue gently from her arms. With great care he and a few soldiers placed him on horseback. Omar's people took charge of the animal and the body. Aaliyah held out her hand and Mercy took it. She pulled her into a hug, holding her lover tight. She prayed for Jalil, for Helima the sister of her heart and for those who had lost their life because of her. When they released each other, Aaliyah turned her eyes back to the palace and said one final prayer for the woman she had once called sister but wasn't sure she could anymore.

NINETEEN

Aaliyah and Mercy entered Lockheart through the bone garden that Ko had shown her with Omar and Akil on their heels. Omar's soldiers waited outside the walls. They were hard pressed about it, but they would not defy their King.

The castle halls, if they could still be called that, were littered with rubble. Those walls that remained were gauged and pockmarked, barely standing. Their steps thundered, the only thing louder the anxious trill of birds from the gardens, now flying freely amongst the ruins. Any forces Odessa might have been keeping close had abandoned her. Incongruous with the destruction around them rose the clean, soft scent of flowers, reminding Aaliyah of that first warm bath upon returning home, and Odessa's skin on her skin. She dug her nails into her palm to keep herself focused.

They made their way to the throne room where Odessa waited. She wore a gold gown that cascaded to her feet, her crown high atop her head and her back straight. For all her Empire was crumbling, Odessa looked as beautiful as she had the night of her coronation. Like this was still her birthright, like she had been waiting for everyone else to realize it was what she deserved.

Once, the sight of her would have brought Aaliyah to her

knees.

Now, it reminded Aaliyah of the Old King, seated on his Iron throne when they'd arrived, like a god untouched but for the coup around him. Odessa had buried his throne beneath the earth. Aaliyah wondered what would happen now.

"What took you so long?" Odessa asked with a smile on her face.

Mercy moved forward, but Aaliyah stopped her. She approached the throne on her own. Odessa stopped her with a stone wall that shot up and then receded.

"Right there is close enough. I know what you're about, kingslayer," Odessa said.

"You sound paranoid, O," Mercy said, trying to compose herself. Odessa's nostrils flared. She returned her attention to Aaliyah.

"Do you know there were people who told me that you would betray me? There were people who told me that you wanted the kingdom for yourself? But did I listen? No. I protected you, always," Odessa said. "And this is how you repay me?"

Aaliyah clenched her fist, willing her anger into submission. "And where are those people now?"

The silence hung heavy between them. Odessa's jaw clenched and she swallowed. She stood up, stepping down from her throne. She still looked like the King they'd killed, posturing and desperate.

"I see you decided to get involved in my affairs after all, Omar," Odessa said.

"Only when it seemed you couldn't handle them yourself," King Omar said.

Odessa's eyes flickered over Akil, her head tilting. "I'll tell you what. You take Aaliyah and her merry band here into custody, and I will give you a piece of my empire. Your first kiss with Akil was in the Karden Isles, wasn't it? You could have those. An excellent present after such a terrible adventure."

"You'll forgive me, Odessa, but you sound desperate," Omar said.

"Thirsty even," Akil said.

Odessa shrugged. "It was a kindness I was offering. A way

out."

"But I've seen your people, Odessa. They don't want you," Omar said. Odessa's nostril's flare again. "They want her."

"Mages!" Odessa called. None answered her call. It hurt to watch Odessa realize just how alone she was.

"They aren't coming," Aaliyah said. "There is no one left."

"My champion," Odessa said looking at Aaliyah again. "End this, love."

"I intend to," Aaliyah said. "Abdicate the throne and you can survive this night."

"Like hell she will," Mercy hissed.

"Abdicate the throne and you can go off on your own. Perhaps Oxnar will take you," she said.

"Aaliyah, you have to end her. I told you before," Mercy snarled. "If they'll steal once they can't be trusted not to do it again."

"Get your bitch under control," Odessa said coolly.

Mercy twisted out of Aaliyah's hold and surged forward. Stone spires flew out of the ground, stopping her progress. She was nearly impaled but Aaliyah drew her back again. Mercy pulled away from her.

"I'll make you a deal. Get rid of your whore and we can rule this kingdom together," Odessa said. "I'll even let you keep Helima."

Aaliyah took a deep breath as the stone spires retreated back into the ground. She considered her next words carefully. "Odessa, you have starved and abandoned your people, you have named your sister a traitor, you killed a man you've known for years, but the thing you care about most right now is keeping your crown and getting rid of Mercy. Am I right?"

"You make it sound bad when you say it like that." Odessa gave her a sick smile.

"Last chance."

"Fuck. You."

Aaliyah balanced her spear and hurled it, but Odessa blocked it with a wall. She used the distraction to run forward, charging into Odessa as the wall fell. Odessa twisted away, raising a spire that impaled Aaliyah's leg. Aaliyah bit back a scream as the spire fell away and retrieved her spear. She swung it like a staff, knocking Odessa to her knees. Another spire rose up but fell as Odessa cried out. Mercy's hand clenched, grasping Odessa's bones beneath her flesh and pulling them toward the surface. Odessa's agonized bellows rung against the throne room's walls.

Odessa dragged stones from the ceiling, nearly burying Mercy beneath them, but Helima pushed her out of the way. Aaliyah hadn't noticed Helima's return. Aaliyah raised herself up, ignoring the protest from her left leg, and limped towards Odessa. Her sister drew another spire but Aaliyah was ready. She rolled along the side of the spire, using the momentum to throw her forward. She raised her spear high and Odessa's eyes went round with fear. Aaliyah brought the spear down, impaling Odessa through her heart. Odessa spasmed and the ground twitched in response.

The spire fell away into the earth, as did the stone throne, leaving behind an empty dais. As she had done when they'd killed the old king, Aaliyah said a small prayer to the gods. Despite everything, she asked them to give Odessa peace in death. It was only right.

Aaliyah let herself fall then. Let herself lay beside Odessa for the very last time. She closed her eyes for just a moment, just to get her bearings in the dark behind her eyes. She heard a voice, whispering that she loved her. That she was safe. That they were finally safe.

EPILOGUE

When she opened her eyes again she was in a bed. It wasn't her room but it had a similar layout. Mercy slept beside her, curled up on top of the blankets. Aaliyah sat up, her leg throbbing in protest. Akil, Jalil and Omar were sitting by the fire whispering to each other. Her heart seized at the sight of her friend.

Aaliyah cleared her throat and they all came over to her. Jalil handed her a glass of water and Aaliyah drank it down. When she handed him back the glass she noticed Mercy's eyes were open. The other woman sat up, stretching and yawning exaggeratedly.

"How do you feel?" Akil asked.

"Like the dead risen. What happened?" Aaliyah said.

"You nearly died," Mercy said.

"You had half the kingdom in terror," Jalil said with a little smile.

"Not a very good first act as Queen," Omar said. "You're very lucky that Mercy can heal as well as she can destroy."

"How are the people?" Aaliyah asked. Mercy smiled, taking Aaliyah's hand in hers.

"We fed them on your behalf and we have the mages that remain working on shelter for the homeless. I hope you don't mind," Mercy said.

"I don't. Where's Helima? Sherrod?"

Jalil looked down at his feet. "Helima has charged herself with getting the army back into shape."

"And Sherrod has taken on managing the mages for you," Mercy said. "He's doing an excellent job of keeping them in line."

"Did...has anyone burned the body?"

"In the square for all to see. They chanted your name," Akil said quietly.

Aaliyah closed her eyes. She had a few tears left to shed for her sister it seemed. They would have to wait.

"If I may make a recommendation?" Omar said.

"Yes, your Highness?" Aaliyah said, raising an eyebrow.

"Rest first. Mercy seems to know your mind well enough. Let her make arrangements for a coronation and allow Akil and I to make some recommendations about your advisers. Though your friends here seem to be quite adept. You will start your reign better healed than half dead."

"Not friends, your highness," Aaliyah said, "My family. And you'll forgive me but that doesn't sound like me. Jalil, get me Helima and Sherrod and get your ledgers. We have work to do."

Aaliyah's stomach still twisted at the thought of being Queen. She was a soldier. But that had to be better for Titus than a Queen consumed by power. And she had her family to keep her humble. She looked from Akil to Mercy. New *and* old.

Even if Aaliyah didn't know how to do this yet, she would learn.

About the Author

Eboni Dunbar is a queer, black woman who writes queer and black speculative fiction. She resides in the San Francisco Bay Area with her partner. She received her BA from Macalester College and her MFA in Creative Writing from Mills College. She is a VONA Alum, an associate editor for *PodCastle*, an acquiring editor for *FIYAH Literary Magazine* and a freelance reviewer. Her work can be found in *FIYAH*, *Drabblecast*, *Anathema: Spec from the margins* and *Nightlight Podcast*. She can be found online at www.ebonidunbar.com and on Twitter as @sugoionna87.

About the Press

Neon Hemlock is an emerging purveyor of queer chapbooks and speculative fiction. Learn more at www.neonhemlock.com and on Twitter at @neonhemlock.